UNITY

Copyright © 2026 Flash Kitterson
Cover Illustration: Cogtypelawbot

For permission requests, contact flashthecat3@gmail.com

The story, all names, characters, and incidents portrayed in thisproduction are fictitious. No identification with actual persons (living ordeceased), places, buildings, and products is intended or should be inferred.

ISBN: 978-1-965229-04-0 (Paperback)

PROLOGUE

Penlight Forest's early morning air was sharp and cool – breezing about Umi's ears and gray hair as she moved between leaves, bushes, and fallen branches. In one hand the opossum held the leash to her hounds, who strode out ahead of her with their noses dutifully to the ground, and in the other she cradled a lightly mewling savannah kitten – Unity – over the crook of her shoulder.

The atmosphere of the trails was tranquil as a whole, and came as somewhat of a relief to Umi after the weeks she and Harmony had spent in the house caring for the baby. Yet the longer she found herself following the hounds, the more her ease and enjoyment slowly began to fade into idle concern. *Did she really get this much of a head start?*

This feeling was brought to a sharp point after about twenty minutes, when Unity suddenly stopped mewling, and made a slight grumbling noise. Before Umi could glance down and identify what had caused the shift in the kitten's mood, however, her hounds suddenly began to pull sharply – barking, and scrambling on the forest floor.

Struggling to keep up with only one hand on the leash, the opossum staggered after the magical beasts past copse after copse of trees, until they broke out into a particularly large clearing filled with...

Absolutely nothing.

Umi sighed loudly – glancing down to see if Unity was okay before shaking her head at her hounds, who were now standing still. "Stop getting distracted. Have you been leading me after some rabbit all this time?"

The opossum sighed and pulled on the hounds' leash, preparing to reprimand them and set them back on course. But then her gaze wandered between the nearby trees, and she saw it. A body. Face up on a patch of violently disheveled, muddy ground with both arms outspread.

Harmony.

Immediately dismissing her hounds into nothing, Umi jolted forward to kneel behind her lover with a wail of shock – running the back of her hand along the matted, ruffled fur of Harmony's cheek. Unity began to cry amidst her mother's sharp, urgent movements, but the opossum took no measure to calm her for now, and instead focused all her magic and all her senses towards desperately searching for some sign of life.

Her panic only intensified further when she found none - nor traces of what had happened to the cat. There was no blood around her form, no clearly artificial marks upon her clothes, and no signs of a struggle despite the ruined state of the forest ground. And yet, in that moment... Umi knew exactly what had happened.

She was so strong, for so long. But she couldn't... even she couldn't...

Raising her head with tears streaking down her cheeks, Umi closed her eyes, and began to channel the power within her. Soon, the air of the forest became wild – brushing trees to and fro violently as energy amassed, creatures fled and the silhouette of a wyvern was cast down upon the opossum woman, her child, and her fallen lover.

"Elderex. Take us to the city."

The week before the funeral was a silent and solemn one. Destiny and Kijury immediately ordered a standstill to the palace's business upon learning of what had happened, and invited Umi to stay at the palace so that she could grieve in safety while Harmony's body was examined, and preparations were made.

What felt like almost half of Penlight City's population assembled both within and without the city's church when the day itself came – bearing flowers, material gestures of respect, and teary eyes. Those who Harmony had helped, whose lives she had protected as a knight of the kingdom, and who had known her, personally or otherwise.

Once the ceremony had run its course and the majority of those attending had departed, Umi found herself knelt on the smooth stone in front of Harmony's gray and gold casket – a sleeping Unity in her arms, and tears running down her cheeks.

I'll miss you, Harmony. But I'll keep our daughter safe. As best as I can.

At that moment, Umi felt a hand on her shoulder, and turned to see Destiny's tall, black-clad form standing over her – the bulge of pregnancy just barely visible through her regal attire.

They'd spent a lot of time in one another's company over the past week, as Umi had struggled to take care of both herself and Unity through the grief, but something felt different about seeing the Queen in a setting like this, with the high ceiling of the church framed behind her. She seemed noble, powerful, and yet... broken too, in a way.

And when she spoke, it was clear that Destiny, too, was holding back the strength of her emotions. "I know all too well that nothing can ever replace her, Umi. That she will always be... missing, in a way. But we're here for you and Unity – I need you to know that. Myself, Kijury, and the entire kingdom, if need be."

Umi stayed silent for a long moment, before finally nodding and rising to her feet – being careful not to jostle Unity out of her rest in the process. "Thank you, my lady. Your guidance means a lot to me, as it did to Harmony. Although..."

She sighed deeply, and looked down at her daughter lying in her arms. "It won't be all that long before you have your own new set of responsibilities. I don't want to weigh upon you as well. I can manage."

Destiny opened her mouth to respond, but the clack of gentle footsteps on tile came at that moment, and both women turned to see Kijury and Yuuto approaching from amongst the pews. Kijury was dressed in black robes, and Yuuto as well – though the latter still bore his characteristic horned mask.

When Kijury drew near, he bowed solemnly in Umi's direction, and shook his head. "We will manage. And we trust you. To do what is right, and what is best for both yourself and Unity."

The deer's eyes rose, and locked with the opossum's. "Harmony trusted you too."

Umi didn't say anything more. She couldn't. Instead, she simply nodded, and turned to the side – bidding Harmony's sleek coffin one last glance.

I'm so lost without you, my love.

In many ways, the following year was like any other. The winter came and passed, the fields flourished, and the folk went about their rituals and trades with the same tireless dedication that they had ever since their births at Ophin's hands.

Yet in others, it was a year of great change. Destiny gave birth to two twin girls, and the kingdom celebrated – lauding both, once more, the love between the Queen and her loyal protector, and the future heirs to the Penlight throne.

As for Umi… it is often said that time heals all wounds, but for the opossum, her sensations of loss and hopelessness only deepened as the months went by. For a while her perseverance was only fueled further by the grief she felt, but after the fatigue of motherhood began to wear her thin, thick cracks in her mind and spirit began to form. She cried herself to sleep every night, and every time she glanced upon her savannah cat daughter, she could only see Harmony's face.

Before long, and before the next summer set itself fully into effect, the sadness had almost fully taken her. Longing for the end replaced any hope she'd had, she lost herself to frantically trying to take care of Unity where she could, and alongside it came an avalanche of shame – for feeling as though she had failed her lover, for failing, and for every time that she found herself forced to turn to Destiny and Kijury for assistance.

Eventually, after a long, stormy night where the tears and visions of all that had been lost were stronger than ever, the dam broke. The only thing keeping Umi back from the brink of losing herself completely was knowing that without her, Unity would be alone, but she also knew that things couldn't continue this way.

She left what had been her and Harmony's house, that morning, and made her way across the city with a sleeping Unity in her arms, and a cloak upon her shoulders to cover her face. Not towards the castle – for no, she would not allow the Queen to suffer under her burden, or to know of her deep weakness just yet - but towards the orphanage just beyond the edge of the city walls.

It was a squat but elegant building surrounded by a modest garden, two small towers, and an outstretched wing of the Penlight forest. Umi made across the cobblestones with a glance to and fro to make sure she wasn't being followed, took one last deep breath, and opened the orphanage's front door to move inside.

There, she found an ornate entry hall, decorated with a tiled floor, wooden furniture, and – at its center – a desk with a female golden retriever sat behind it. The retriever's ears and head perked up at the new arrival, and she smiled warmly at both Umi and the bundle in her arms. "Welcome to the Penlight Orphanage! Miss...?"

Umi bowed her head, stood there in the center of the tiles. "Hoshi."

The retriever stood, moved forward to close the distance, and reached out to shake Umi's free hand. "Nice to meet you! My name is Angel Harper. Is that your child?"

Now the opossum nodded. "Yes. Her name is Unity Tsuki Mei. And I'm... giving her up for adoption."

A brief look of sadness, worry, and defeat flashed behind Ms. Harper's eyes, but then she set her warm smile back in place. "Oh! What a pretty name! And what makes you want to leave her in our care?"

Unity, who seemed to have been woken by the conversation, babbled a little at that moment, and Umi felt a tear prick in the corner of her eye as she resisted the urge to look down at her. "I'm... not fit. To be her mother. And I'm scared. That I do harm, to her, to myself..."

She sighed, and her gaze dropped. She wasn't able to say this to this woman's face, despite just having met her. "Her mother... my lover... died. And without her, I... can't. I've tried – for a year, I have. But I can't. I know that it's time."

Angel stayed silent for a few seconds after Umi finished, before finally nodding with a deeply solemn air. "I see. Please – come take as a seat. We'll talk this over, just to make sure this is the right decision, and so that you can express how you'd like us to handle things."

Umi complied, and followed the retriever into a smaller room with a set of couches, wide bay windows, and flowers set in small pots along every corner. The building seemed quiet, clean, and well maintained, and there were bookshelves filled with books everywhere she looked.

This... seems like a nice place. And this woman seems lovely. Maybe... there really is hope here.

A few hours later, however, with the deed done, tearful goodbyes said, and last assurances received, the opossum could not have felt less certain. Standing out front of the orphanage, where clouds had since started to amass and the first drops of rain were beginning to fall from the sky, she tugged her cloak back over herself, held her chin high, and began to make off back through the city with tears streaking openly down her face.

We'll cross paths again someday, Unity. I know we will. I may have failed you, but... I trust the power of your blood. That you'll grow strong. Just like your mother.

But not like me.

Across the city in the halls of the Queen's palace, however, the atmosphere and scene could not have been more different - loud, chaotic, and tinged with exhausted resignation.

The sound of infantile crying echoed throughout the stones surrounding Destiny's boudoir, and within, the white linen-dressed Queen herself could barely hear her own thoughts for fatigue.

While Destiny busied herself cradling and hushing Amethyst – brown-furred, with round ears - who she'd recently plucked out of her crib, Kijury knelt near the bed, where their other daughter, Justice, lay. Justice wasn't screaming, unlike her sister, but had instead pulled her blond-furred, antler-crowned face into a scowl, and seemed mere seconds from joining in.

"Oh, come on... This usually gets you two!" Kijury, who had been pulling entertaining faces and making cooing sounds, let out a sigh and turned back to glance over at his wife. "Only you have luck with this, these days."

Destiny smirked a little through her exhaustion. "Didn't you train Harmony, Irin, and Umi?"

"They don't count. They weren't babies."

The lean hound woman chuckled a little at that, and as a result, Amethyst finally stopped screaming – instead looking up at her mother with an unsteady, disoriented gaze.

Moving gently, Destiny set her daughter back down in the crib, just as Justice slumped down on the sheets of the bed, and Kijury turned about with a breath of relief. No sooner had he done so, however, than he found his wife face to face with him – a tired but genuine smile across her muzzle. "But you are an amazing father, nonetheless. Even though they inherited your energy."

Kijury blushed, and embraced her. "Oh, hush, you."

Destiny returned the embrace warmly, feeling herself sinking into her husband's arms with almost enough satisfaction to start falling asleep right away.

Yet, despite that long-awaited calm, something had her ill at ease. Their life was so... simple right now, with the knights taking over most of the duties around the castle, and although their current tasks had them at their limits in a way that ruling the kingdom never could, the Queen couldn't help but recall that things wouldn't be this way forever.

The future of Penlight was uncertain – powerfully, tumultuously so – and with each hour, conflict and evil power grew both without and within the many corners of its reach. War, magic, and danger unbounded. So much was at stake. So much had already been lost.

And – someday – these small, fragile, innocent girls would bear the sole responsibility for it all.

1

— . —

Fifteen years later

While the halls, dormitories, and old-style floors of Penlight Orphanage were robust and ornate, they could not fully abate or contain the raucous nature of its three-score inhabitants – youths of all ages, species, and dispositions.

Least of all when it came to Unity Mei.

Over the course of her fifteen years at the orphanage, Unity had quickly developed a reputation as a self-isolating and sometimes unruly child, and this reputation often caused most of the caretakers and other children to either clash with her or, at best, pay her as little mind as possible.

The sole exception to this rule was the house's head - Ms. Harper. After noting the reluctance of her staff when it came to giving Unity the care she needed, the golden retriever had taken to watching after the girl almost as though she were her personal charge. Where the rest of the orphanage shunned the gray, spotted cat girl, Ms. Harper showed her nothing but love – checking in on her regularly, and sitting with her on some of her many lonely evenings.

It was on one partially lonely evening, about a month after her sixteenth birthday, that Unity found herself sat on the balustrade of the orphanage's attic balcony - watching the sun sink to tease the tree line of the forest beyond the grounds. About her shoulders, flowing down to cover her form, she wore a black sundress emblazoned with the dark blue and white outlines of tentacles – her latest gift from Ms. Harper, and the only one she had received for her birthday.

She came here often, as a last refuge to escape the scowls and sharp jabs of the other children - and even Ms. Harper's well-intentioned doting, if she was feeling particularly reclusive. And this day was definitely one of those occasions. The feeling of isolation amongst hateful eyes was even more overwhelming than it usually was, and even the gentle afternoon breeze could do little to ease her own dark, bitter mood.

It felt like she'd been here in this state, unanimously decided as too 'different' and 'prickly' by all parties around her, for her entire life. Barely anyone even spoke to her - even Ms. Harper was too busy with a new arrival to the orphanage to sit with her tonight - and the time where she'd be expected to enter the world as an adult was approaching rapidly.

They'll be worse, out there, won't they? More stuck-up. More stupid.

The cat girl scoffed and pulled herself forward with a familiar shift of her body weight – slipping down to first hang from the outside of the balustrade by both arms, and then to drop to the third floor balcony beneath it with all the agility her felinity afforded her. *I don't need them, anyway. Any of them. I'm Unity, and I'm amazing all on my own.*

At first she was preoccupied with righting herself and brushing off the back of her dress, but then the sound of stifled snickering drifted in from behind her, and her ears perked up in annoyance. *It isn't them, is it?*

A quick jerk of her head confirmed her fears, and brought a deep grimace to her features. *Great. Just what I needed.*

Stood up against the entrance to the hall beyond the balcony, leant up against the old wooden chairs that lined the wooden floor, was a lion, jaguar, and an eagle – all about a year older than Unity, dressed in unkempt dark clothes, and all watching her with high noses and sinister smirks.

Though her face remained defiant, Unity's heart sunk in frustration. King, Ron, and Darvell – the orphanage's absolute worst specimens. Smug, antagonistic, and apparently omnipresent. These idiots didn't usually come up here, but from the expressions on their faces, it was clear that they were in a particularly troublesome mood.

By the time that Unity fully wheeled about and brought herself to stand straight and defiant, King took a step forward, and his smirk turned into a sneer.

"Look what we have here." He jerked his head upwards. "Hey, pussy. Looking for mice up there? For company, of course."

The insult was base and stupid, but it made Unity bear her teeth nonetheless. *And I was having such a peaceful evening. Better a wall's company than any of you.*

Unity took a step forward of her own, and threw out her arms. "What do you want, *Queen*? Are you really this boring? Nothing better to do?"

That made King growl, and his two lackeys echo a mocking 'ooh' sound. Unity knew teasing him was dangerous, cornered as she was, but she'd never had the best grasp of restraint.

"My name is *King*, pathetic kitten. Ron?" The lion gestured over his shoulder to the jaguar without taking his gaze off of Unity. "I think we found just what we were looking for."

The other feline moved forward with a wicked grin, and King advanced as well – edging closer and closer towards the balustrade where Unity stood in a defensive stance. "I thought you might have learned your lesson the last time we beat your ass. But never mind – unlike you, repeats of this never get boring."

Unity opened her mouth to snarl back yet another insult, fight-ready adrenaline already surging through her veins, but King was even more bloodthirsty than she'd expected – moving forward to first feigned with a punch, and then sweep his leg out to catch the cat girl completely unaware.

She'd been far from unprepared, but her balance being torn out from underneath her was enough to make Unity cry out in surprise – just barely catching herself on the balustrade to save herself from going down completely. *D-damn it! In a fair fight, I'd have all three of them in a second.*

That one second of disorientation was all that Ron needed to close the space between them, with Darvell not long behind – whooping and joining in as King began to lash out again and again with his foot, impacting first Unity's legs, and then even her side as she struggled to get back onto her feet.

At first Unity simply gritted her teeth and readied a roar – building up energy in her body to leap forward and tackle Ron to burst out from being backed against the edge of the balcony – but just before she could power forward, a high voice came from the door behind them.

"King! Ron! Darvell!"

The three thugs froze at that – even King - and turned around on a dime to look in the direction of the voice. It was Ms. Harper – stood in the doorway separating the balcony from the hall in a blue casual shirt and trousers, and with a furious look on her face.

Even Unity stayed perfectly still, arms braced against the balustrade, as a moment of silence passed before Ms. Harper spoke. "You boys go to your room. All of you – and don't leave until we've had enough talk."

King's face fell – though not in aggression, now, but rather annoyance and impertinence. "But, Ms. Harper, she-"

Ms. Harper shook her golden-furred head sharply, cutting the lion short. "No buts, King. Off to your room, now."

Another moment of tense silence passed, before the three boys sighed and took a few steps away from Unity – though they still cast a dark, resentful glance back at her before filing past Ms. Harper in the doorway and moving on out of sight.

Heart still beating hard, Unity righted herself properly, and wiped at the side of her head, where her cheek had banged against wood. *They couldn't even do the damage themselves. Pathetic.*

Ms. Harper approached, hand already reaching to her side to produce a handkerchief, but the cat girl refused to meet her eyes. "I had that under control."

Stopping short and bridging her hands on her hips, Ms. Harper sighed gently. "I'm sure you did, Unity. I know you can watch out for yourself. But as much as I condemn their behavior, you must be more careful. I won't always be around if you are in over your head."

Unity didn't respond. She hadn't thought about that before, and had nothing to say that wouldn't feel like losing face.

Before the silence could stretch any longer, however, Ms. Harper continued her approach, until she drew Unity up into a tight hug – stroking at her white hair lovingly. "I understand. Go get yourself cleaned up, alright? The cook is still busy in the kingdom tonight, so you'll have to get yourself a sandwich from the kitchen. The other kids should be done by now – you'll have some peace, at least. Except…"

Ms. Harper tilted her head down against Unity's shoulder, and lowered her voice a little. "As you know, I wasn't able to come to our usual chat because I was welcoming a new arrival. I will have time for tomorrow, of course – but I told our new arrival to wait in the kitchen for someone to come help her with food, and I'd like it very much if you were able to help her feel at least a little welcome, alright?"

Unity raised her head and frowned. *First she leaves me alone, and now I need to go play greeting party?* "Do I have to?"

Ms. Harper tilted her head, and raised a hand to run along the cat girl's sore cheek appraisingly. "It'd be very kind of you, Unity. I know you have it in you."

Too tired from the altercation to object, the cat girl nodded reluctantly, and stepped back out of the embrace. Ms. Harper trailed away with one last worried glance in her green eyes, before turning heel and making back through the doorway through which she had come – leaving little more than her golden silhouette cast in the evening light behind her.

Unity hesitated for a moment before following – sighing deeply, and reaching up to cradle her injury.

As miserable and pessimistic as she still felt, faced with a task she could have wanted to do less, and the thought of having to face King and his gang time and time again for Ophin knows how long… She couldn't deny that Ms. Harper being there for her, or at least trying to, made the orphanage at least a little more tolerable. *She certainly loves me more than any of them ever did.*

More than my mother did.

A few minutes later, Unity finished up washing up her face and the bruise on her cheek in the bathroom, and made to leave back into the hallway – though not without casting one last glance at herself in the old, round mirror above the sink.

Her pale-white hair. Her gray fur, with its pattern of spots. The black fabric of her dress, which looked a little worse for wear after the fight earlier. *Just look at me. No wonder the others hate me so much.*

Before she could move through the doorway, however... something entirely unexpected happened. Cold like claws gripped at her back in the space of a second, the faint light filtering through the building's windows seemed to dim. And, most strikingly of all, then it came – the voice. Drifting in from all around, almost as though it were directly within her skull.

Hate you? For now. But soon they will come to fear you.

The cat girl froze, and glanced back behind her urgently – preparing for King or one of his lackeys to be standing there, ready to heckle her. "Who the-"

Nobody. Not in the bathroom, nor in the hallway. And yet the voice returned. *You know, this isn't the first time we've spoken – but you must have forgotten. That's alright – I think we'll have more than enough time to get reacquainted.*

A touch of light fear creeping into her voice as she glanced back and forth and crouched down into a ready stance, Unity snarled. "Whoever you are – you're pathetic, that's not funny."

Yet the voice remained as omnidirectional and invisible as ever. *Trouble's coming, Unity. You'll see. You'll need us soon enough.*

After those final words, the moment was over. The darkness and cold was gone, just like that – leaving Unity stood stiffly in the bathroom doorway, and wondering whether she'd felt them at all.

The cat girl straightened and huffed in agitation, wasting no time in picking her pace back up. "Stupid fucking King." *It must have been him. Nobody else would try to mess with me like that.*

A few sighed breaths later, the cat girl had made her way down the carpeted hallway and stepped into the kitchen – a long, narrow room with classic white and black tiling, sets of tables in the middle, a set of cabinets along one wall, and communal stovetops along the other.

Unity had been hoping to be alone for at least a little while longer, despite Ms. Harper's request, but it didn't take long for her to be disappointed. A small rabbit girl around three years younger than her was sat at one of the tables with a sandwich in her hands – although she'd currently paused eating, and had turned about to stare at Unity with ears piqued high.

The cat girl didn't remember the rabbit's name, but she scowled and huffed nonetheless – still agitated and on edge from the voice speaking to her. "What're you looking at? Shouldn't you be out in the garden eating carrots or something, rabbit?"

That was enough to flatten the rabbit's ears and send her screeching back in her chair – hastily steadying herself before rounding the tables and counter to leave with sandwich in hand, making sure to keep as much distance as possible from Unity as she did so.

Unity continued to scowl after as the other girl disappeared through the doorway she had just entered. "Come on! It was only a joke!"

"I don't think she liked the joke."

At first the cat girl was frightened that the voice had returned, but upon turning to track the direction the sound had come from, she found a figure sat against the short, horizontal wall, out of view from where she'd entered. It was a snake – older than the rabbit girl, and dressed in the simple gray blouse and trousers that all of the orphanage's children were given. Her face was narrow, her scales dull, and her expression unreadable.

At first Unity readied a sigh and another biting comment, but the second that their gazes met, the snake's dark purple eyes looked deep into Unity's muddy green ones, and she found herself freezing up. There was something dark behind that violet – something not altogether threatening, but foreboding nonetheless, and even a little... familiar?

Trouble's coming, Unity. You'll see. You'll need us soon enough.

The snake's cold, uninflected tone returned. "I said – I don't think she liked the joke."

Unity shook her head, almost snarling as she fought to keep herself from showing her surprise. Turning about with a huff, she pulled open one of the kitchen cabinets, snatched out a half-eaten loaf of round bread, and thudded it onto the counter. "Thanks. I couldn't tell."

Seizing a jagged knife, the cat girl began to saw off a few slices, perhaps more aggressively than she should have, and spoke without looking up. "So you're the new girl. And why did your parents not want you?"

A half-drawn breath came from the snake girl's direction, and Unity wondered whether she'd offended the newcomer. *Not like there's any other way to end up here, though. Mine definitely didn't want me. No use sugarcoating it.*

But when the snake spoke again, there was no offense or vitriol in her voice. Nor any other emotions to take note of. "I... never knew my parents."

She stood, revealing herself to be just a little taller than Unity, and took a few steps forward while watching Unity's cutting intently. "The last family I was with said they were too scared to let me stay any longer, and Ms. Harper couldn't find anyone else. Can't blame them."

The other girl's serpentine frame finally drew near enough that Unity stopped slicing, and finally looked up. From this close, she could see the deep color of the snake's eyes even better – and smell her, too. Over the plain wash scent of her simple clothes, the girl smelled floral, almost. Which was strange, given the flat appearance of her scales.

The snake tilted her head while Unity examined her. "Is your hair naturally white?"

That stole away Unity's curiosity, and brought a bitter scowl back to her face. *Does everyone need to poke at me and remind me of how different I am?* "Uh... yeah. Ms. Harper told me it is, at least."

She dropped the knife altogether, and held out a hand in the snake's direction. *Speaking of Ms. Harper, might as well give what she asked a shot.* "Unity. Unity T. Mei."

The snake looked down at the offered grasp for a long moment, almost looking perplexed, but then took it and shook it. "Michelle Exousia."

Unity shrugged at that, and turned away to take the bread she'd cut over to the pantry, where she was able to produce some thin cuts of meat and cheese. "So, Michelle Exousia – are you hungry? Might as well eat, if you're set on being here."

Michelle nodded, and Unity began to make a sandwich both for herself and the other girl while she watched.

It didn't take long for the snake's next question to arrive. "Where are all the others?"

Putting a final slice of cheese on the second sandwich, Unity raised both eyebrows. "They ate already. But isn't it better being alone?"

Michelle seemed to think for a long while, even as Unity handed her her sandwich, but eventually she nodded. "I think so. It is."

Unity couldn't help but smile a little at that, albeit bitterly. *Well, now. She's better than a brick wall, at least.*

They leant against the counter and began to eat in silence from then on, much to Unity's enjoyment. She hadn't found sharing a meal this enjoyable – or at least tolerable – for as long as she could remember.

Maybe Ms. Harper's precious new arrival isn't so bad after all.

2

— . —

Some weeks passed after Michelle's arrival, taking Penlight Orphanage and the forest surrounding it into the buzzing heart of spring.

Carts full of produce trundled back and forth along the roads to and from the building, Ms. Harper readied their funding books to calculate stores for the year, and the children even shared an outing to the castle for the harvest festival. Even Unity had tagged along – although only at Ms. Harper's persistent pleading.

Although, in the end, she'd soon found it to be just as dull and isolating as she'd expected. The decorations and crowded streets were interesting in comparison to the orphanage's empty halls, yes, but she hadn't had a single coin to buy anything from any of the stalls, and none of the other children had so much as looked her way the entire time.

Except Michelle.

At first, Unity had scoffed at the idea that now, after all these years of relative isolation, she could have someone that seemed to like her company. But when what was at first coincidence and Unity trying her best to be 'welcoming' as per Ms. Harper's wishes soon turned into somewhat of a routine, it became clear that she actually enjoyed Michelle's company too.

The snake was cold and quiet most of the time, sure, but she was honest, didn't judge the cat girl for her other moods, and was never reluctant to listen to Unity's complaints or musings about the orphanage and its other occupants.

After around three weeks had passed since Michelle's arrival, and a week since they'd walked through the streets of the castle together, Unity and Michelle found themselves using up a free midday sitting atop the orphanage's balcony, with the former dressed in her black sundress as always. Which was no small ordeal – this space was Unity's private, secret refuge of sorts, and she'd never shared her spot up here with anyone before. Not even Ms. Harper.

Their talk was sparse but sincere, as it had tended to be over their short time in each other's company, but Unity didn't mind. The gaps in conversation gave her time to look over the orphanage's grounds and watch the children playing or likewise conversing below them, as well as dwell on her own thoughts and the noises of nature around them.

The cat girl even found herself smiling at one point – caught by surprise by an almost-joke Michelle had made. *She's really not so bad after all. Why on earth didn't her last family want her?*

But she's nothing next to what you could be, Unity.

The intrusion upon her thoughts caused Unity to jolt upright from leaning against the balcony's balustrade – ears tense, and eyes wide. All her peace and relaxation was gone in an instant. "Did you hear that?"

"Hear what?" Turning to regard Unity with confusion, Michelle tilted her head to the side.

Unity waited for a long moment in silence, listening, before shaking her head at hearing nothing more than the birds of the forest and the wind. "I... don't know. Maybe I just need a nap." She frowned, and looked about them at the children below again. "I'm bored of looking at them anyway. We should go someplace else."

Michelle nodded, and the two backed away from the balcony. Just as the two made to turn around, however, a snickering noise came from behind them, and the pair of girls froze.

Unity's face darkened. *So we're not alone after all.*

"Well, well, well. What have we here?"

The cat girl knew it was King long before she finally came about to see him – standing there surrounded, as usual, by his lackeys, framed by the door behind him just as he had been on the day that Michelle had arrived.

Except, this time was different. King had never bothered her up here, which was one of the reasons she had come up here so often. And the thought that her one refuge in the entire orphanage had been violated was enough to send a surge of anger through Unity's body stronger than anything she'd felt in a long while. She seethed. *Who do they think they are?*

That, however, was when she noticed something in each of the three's hands. Rocks – they must be. Her anger darkened to fear. *They mean business this time.*

Almost as though he sensed Unity's sudden trepidation, King's sneer widened, and he stepped forward. "Ms. Harper is out in the kingdom getting supplies until the afternoon, and you know what that means." Another step closer. "Nobody around to save you. Or your snake friend."

That last part stumped Unity – even more than the impending threat of the three thugs. Half of her wanted to refute the lion's words with *'she's not my friend'* or something similar, but as much as her reflex snapped, her mouth and mind failed to comply. *I guess she is.*

Before she could come up with a response, however, there was another brush of movement, and the cat girl flinched – half expecting one of the stones to have been thrown. When she looked over, however, she found that it was in fact Michelle, who had stepped forward to match King's advance.

The snake's expression was as neutral as always, and when she spoke it was with an equally uninflected tone. But about her... was a kind of dark blur that made Unity blink over and over again in confusion.

"You three should leave. I don't want to hurt you."

Unity's expression turned to one of confusion and worry. *She's taking them head-on? I don't think we have much of a chance, with nowhere to go.*

King, too, seemed bewildered by the snake's words – spreading his arms threateningly and scoffing. "And who do you think you are, snake? Maybe you just don't know your place yet."

He smiled over his shoulder to his lackeys. "Let's get her!"

One heartbeat later, and all three of the thugs raised their arms – taking aim, pulling back, and letting the stones in their palms fly. Unity recoiled as quickly as she could, raising her own arm to guard her face and preparing for the pain of impact, but then a second passed, and another...

Eventually, the cat risked a glance up, before gasping out loud at what she saw. The stones were there, alright, but they were simply hanging in the air – suspended by what looked like a dark, foggy field of energy that rippled and waved across the balcony for a good few feet.

Directly before this field stood Michelle – her arm outstretched, and a deep shadow radiating from her eyes that made Unity blink again and again in uncertainty. *Is this... really happening?*

King and his lackeys, too, were frozen staring, and remained in that state even after the energy eventually dissipated, and the rocks fell to clatter upon the wooden boards of the balcony.

Then King took his first step. Back, rather than forwards, with a stammer upon his tongue. "Wh-what the hell are you?"

Michelle lowered her arm, but the glow in her eyes remained. "If you don't want to find out, I suggest you leave us alone."

At first it seemed clear that King's fear would soon bring him to turn tail, but before he could do so or say more, the jaguar by his side snarled out loud and reached down to the ground to pick up another loose piece of slate that had likely once belonged to the roof. "You can't scare us with tricks, Snake. We're gonna beat your asses!"

Before even King could react, the rock was flying again – arcing towards Michelle just as the others' had. Again she raised her arm, and again the stone stopped. But it didn't drop this time – instead flying back towards Ron with almost more speed than it he himself had given it, and striking the jaguar cleanly on the side of the head with a sharp 'thud'.

Another long, almost slow-motion moment of silence drew on as Ron teetered, raised his hand halfway to the place where he had been hit, and then finally toppled over - crashing to the ground with an impact that Unity could feel through the boards under her feet.

As the jaguar dropped, so did King and Darvell's jaws. But the two made no effort to help their friend up whatsoever - instead springing back towards the attic's door and shaking their heads, shoulders hunched as though they expected more projectiles to fly at them at any moment.

"Y-you'll regret t-this!" King's voice was shaky, and the fearful panting under his breath was soon muffled as the lion and his eagle lackey turned heel and fled back through the dusty threshold through which they had entered. Ron wasn't long behind them, after he regained his feet and managed to scramble back across the balcony in turn.

Before long, Unity and Michelle were left alone on the attic balcony - panting a little themselves, and with the cat girl finally glancing back over to check on her friend. Michelle's eyes had returned to normal, and it was almost as though the entire surreal scene had never happened... but Unity could still feel a crackling of energy through the air around her and her very bones, and her heart was still racing in disbelief.

"T-thanks, but... what... was that?"

Michelle turned her head downwards, so that Unity was only able to see the scales of her neck. "I... don't know. I've just always been able to do this – to feel this... power within myself, and sometimes the world too. It's... why my other families didn't want me."

She raised her gaze to meet Unity's once more. "Please don't be scared."

The cat girl thought for a long moment, teetering between awe and confusion, before eventually shaking her head. "I'm not scared."

Michelle smiled. But even as she did, and Unity felt inclined to grin in relief as well, a voice spoke out of nowhere yet again – deeper, darker, and more pervasive than ever before. *That could be you, Unity. You want power, don't you?*

You want to see them fear you too, don't you?

The midday came to an end with little incident, and an almost unearthly quiet throughout the halls and yards of the orphanage. No voices trailed through the air as Unity and Michelle made their way to and from the kitchen for lunch, and only the fleeing tails of a few other orphans were visible in the yard as they came to sit at the edge of its fountain. It was almost as though the news and foreboding energy of Michelle's intimidating performance was spreading, and spreading fast.

Unity didn't exactly mind, of course. She preferred quiet, and the idea that King and his thugs would likely leave them alone for some time now had inspired more than a little bit of gloating from the cat girl amongst her chatter with Michelle. *That'll teach them. For good. Finally I can have a say around this miserable place, and finally I have someone to back me up.*

Maybe things won't end up so bad around here after all.

Yet their relative peace didn't last forever. Just as the sun was beginning to burn a little orange in the sky, and the breeze over the hedges surrounding the fountain began to cool some, a set of footsteps approached from about the corner, and both Unity and Michelle turned to see Ms. Harper approaching from the direction of the orphanage.

The retriever, dressed in a polite white dress, had her hands folded in her lap, and greeted the two girls with a friendly nod as she drew near. "Unity, Michelle. It's a lovely day, isn't it? I just arrived back from the city. We'll be eating well for the next weeks."

The two nodded in unison, and for a moment, Ms. Harper stood in silence – looking them up and down with a gentle but concerned air.

When she did speak, it was slowly and in a quiet, soft tone. "I'm sorry to disturb you two, but I came to find you because I have something important to say. And a few questions." The retriever frowned a little. "First of all - King and his friends came to me again. Only this time, they named you too, Michelle."

Unity glanced over at the snake, expecting to see some kind of reaction on the other girl's face, but Michelle remained completely expressionless and silent as Ms. Harper continued to speak. "I understand and appreciate that you two had to defend yourselves, and I'm glad that you were able to. But... there's something we need to discuss."

The cat girl's gaze returned to her guardian, and her head tilted to the side. "Like what?"

Ms. Harper's mouth drifted open in preparation to speak, but then there was the crunch of rapid footsteps amongst the hedges nearby, and she snapped it shut again as a pair of younger children dashed past giggling, clearly engaged in some kind of play.

By the time that the two had vanished and relative silence had returned to the area surrounding the fountain again, the orphanage caretaker's strangely sincere expression had eased a little, and she cracked a gentle smile. "You know, I'm so glad to see you getting along. Not that I didn't believe that you would, in the end. In fact, the two of you have more in common than you might know."

Now it was Michelle's turn to tilt her head in question. "What do you mean?"

That fresh smile vanished. Ms. Harper unfolded her hands, and began to speak very slowly – eyes seeming even more uncertain than before. "That is what I meant to speak to you about. You are here for your protection. Both of you. And incidents like this... Are dangerous. Could be more dangerous than I can explain."

The retriever focused on Unity, and extended one open hand in her direction. "That means you too, Unity. Fifteen years ago, when you first arrived here, I promised that I would-"

But then it happened. Everyone at once. A flash of bright light, a great, arcane rumble, and the force of a thousand fists knocking Unity up and back, lifting her off of the ground with ease.

By the time that the cat girl felt anything again – the feeling of dirt and wood shoved against her side as she hit the ground – her ears were ringing sharply enough to almost drown out the physical agony throughout her body, and her thoughts were slow and hard-won like after a long midday nap.

What... happened? We were talking, Ms. Harper was telling me something about my arrival, then...

Michelle. Ms. Harper.

Urgency shot through the cat girl's frame, and her limbs followed soon after in jolting straight – pulling her into a frantic kneel.

Yet Unity's first glances to and fro rewarded her with no clarity, and her first breaths brought her only a mouthful of smoky stench. There was no fountain, no hedges, and no orphanage visible amongst the light fog surrounding her. Nothing she recognized at all, in fact – just scraps of leaves and twigs mixed amongst decimated slabs of gray stone piled up to various heights.

Gray like Michelle. Gray like that arm reaching up to-

Unity shoved herself forward towards Michelle's slowly rising figure where it lay between a few larger pieces of wood that she thought she recognized from the orphanage's entry hall - wincing a little as her surely bruised side protested against the sudden motion, but pushing on until she was standing above her dust-covered, disoriented-looking friend.

The cat girl reflexively offered a hand to help Michelle to her feet, but as soon as the snake had brought herself to her knees, she pushed it away and locked eyes with Unity. Her expression had always been stoic, but there was a darkness in it now that Unity couldn't place – like there had been not so long ago, before she had lashed out at King and his minions.

"Stay low. We have to go. Now."

Still trying to catch her breath and organize her thoughts amongst the smoke, and having to train her hearing closely through the ringing still penetrating her ears, Unity balked. "W-why? We need to find Ms. Harper. The others, I... what even happened?"

Now properly on her feet and brushing down her blouse and trousers, Michelle shook her head. "We can't. We need to hide. I feel something - and it doesn't feel right."

Unity glanced around urgently for some explanation to either her earlier questions or Michelle's words, but found none – causing her pulse to rocket higher and higher. *This is a dream, right? Where are all the other children? What happened to the orphanage building?*

But then the swirling fog parted for a moment, and she saw another figure standing not so far away, atop the first patch of unharmed grass she had seen since the explosion. A retriever in a once-white, now black-stained dress, cradling her red-speckled head, and searching about just as Unity had been.

The cat girl turned to Michelle, a relieved smile beaming across her dirty face. "Michelle! There's Ms. Harper! Come on, we have to-"

Yet the snake remained frozen – staring over at where Ms. Harper stood with a stone-like expression that caused Unity to follow her gaze, and freeze in turn at what she saw there.

Ms. Harper was no longer alone, nor was she still looking about herself as though searching for others. Instead, she was backing up with both arms raised – retreating from a slender, tall figure in a dark robe that was approaching her from out of the smog.

Three words reached Unity's ears – echoing with menacing quality despite her dulled hearing.

"Where is she?"

The voice was female, but the power behind it was deep and dread-inducing, and its effects upon Ms. Harper were clear as the retriever shook her head frantically. "They said you'd come. They said..."

The figure advanced further with a pair of long, agile steps, until she stood right before Ms. Harper. The retriever went stock still as a result – gazing up beneath the hood of the figure's robe with nothing but terror written in her eyes

"Of course they did. And they were wise to fear. You, however..."

A thin arm extended slowly from the figure's robes... and then lashed out in the space of a second to grasp at Ms. Harper's yellow-furred throat – casting out a crackle of golden, spark-like energy as it did so. At first the orphanage caretaker only seemed surprised, but then her jaw clenched, and she began to cough as, defying all logic and proportion, her feet rose an inch off of the ground.

The figure tilted her head. "Look what you've brought upon yourself and your children, fool. For what? To protect her, when you are so weak?" She sighed with what sounded like mundane frustration. "Again – I do not have time to waste. Where is she? I can feel her energy. She is living."

At first Ms. Harper could only continue to choke and cough, leaving Unity and Michelle to remain frozen and watching on in horror and anticipation, before the figure let up her grasp a little to allow her to speak. "Tell me where she is, or die."

As soon as she regained some freedom and air, Ms. Harper's expression grew stubborn. "N-never. The children are my l-life – I would rather lose mine than risk theirs."

For a moment the figure arched slightly, seeming to boil in anger, but then its shoulders slumped, and it let out a light, mocking laugh. "Still refusing to be useful? I'll still find it, you know. Even without her. It will be harder, but I'll find the Sun Skewer nonetheless."

Unity hissed back at Michelle, heart thudding harder in her chest than she could ever remember at the sound of Ms. Harper whimpering. "We need to do something – we can't just let her-"

The figure resumed her grip on Ms. Harper's neck, causing her to gurgle more than choke this time, and cutting Unity short. "I *will*. And I *will* burn her kingdom to the ground - starting right where it's most deserved. With Upholder and her lackeys."

Another squeeze and sparkle of golden energy, causing the retriever's struggling to pick up pace in panic, and her eyes to roll back in her skull.

"And, for your interference... with you."

All of a sudden, the struggling stopped, Ms. Harper's body went limp, and an almost otherworldly silence pervaded the ruins of the orphanage for a long, long moment - before the figure opened her grasp, and the retriever's body fell.

Acting on pure instinct as her caretaker's form hit the debris-strewn ground with a dull thud, Unity forced herself to her feet and began to dash towards the scene with tears prickling in her eyes from both her emotions and the smoke. "Ms. Harper!"

As she made her first desperate, stumbling steps, the figure slowly turned her head toward Unity, and for a split second she could see burning, piercing, lava-golden globes beneath her mask's cowl.

But then the cat girl felt an arm loop around her middle and hoist her off the ground completely with almost supernatural strength – causing her vision to blur altogether, and her balance to fail.

A quick glance behind revealed that it was Michelle who had grabbed her. Unity let out a deep hiss. "No! Let me go! I need to help Ms. Harper!"

Yet Michelle's grasp around Unity's body only tightened - almost impossibly so, for the relatively diminutive stature of her form - and she began to move away from the wreckage they'd been hiding behind at speed, ducking and weaving between pieces of wall and roof with uncanny speed until they reached the first few trees that surrounded the yard.

Giving one last-ditch effort at escape with every fraction of strength she had, Unity struggled and writhed - stretching out her arm in the direction of the smoking ruins, where she had seen her guardian fall. "Ms. Harper!"

But there was no turning back. The forest swallowed up more and more of her view, until the leaves and branches had consumed Penlight Orphanage's ruins entirely.

And, with it, everything that Unity had ever known.

3

— · —

"**J**asper! Can't have you sleeping in on such a special day – the world is waiting!"

A hand fell upon Jasper's shoulder and shook him back and forth, causing him to scrunch up his face and pull his sheets tighter about himself. *It can't be time for chores yet, surely...*

It didn't take all that long for his brain to catch up, however, and for a bolt of realization to wrench his eyes open.

That's right - it's my birthday!

Once the young wolf's eyes had adjusted to the morning light streaming in through the window at the end of his bed, he was greeted by the sight of his father's grinning, cheerful face mere inches from his. Jasper's father, Titan, had always been a cheerful wolf, much like his son, but this was unusual enthusiasm even for him.

Smile broadening even further upon noting that Jasper was awake, Titan leaned back to give his son room to sit up in bed and stretch - which he did with nose high, catching the scent of breakfast meat on the air.

Jasper yawned, and donned a smile of his own. "Good morning. Is Mom making breakfast?"

Titan nodded enthusiastically – standing from the edge of the bed to gesture to the bedroom's low, arched doorway. "You bet! How about you come sit down at the table so I can show you a special something while she finishes up!"

That made the young wolf's ears perk up. *A gift? What could it be?* "Alright! I'll be right there."

After his father left him alone for a few minutes to get dressed into his usual leather jerkin and trousers, Jasper made his way out into the house's cozy, window-lined kitchen to find his mother Fantasia bent over a pan upon the crackling stove, and Titan sat at the table with that same broad smile still on his face.

Jasper's mother glanced warmly over her shoulder at his arrival. "Morning, my grown-up boy! Sixteen, huh?"

"Yep!" Jasper beamed, taking up a seat at the table. Not long after he had settled down, however, he noticed an arm-sized, leather-wrapped object in the center of the table, and his head tilted to the side. "What is this?"

Fantasia *hmmed* happily, while Titan moved forward in his own seat to take the object up and unwrap it from its covering. "Why don't you take a look?"

As the older wolf finished revealing the leather's contents, Jasper's eyes slowly widened. Dotted cities, sketched-out waters, and painstakingly illustrated forests stretched out in minute detail revealed themselves. He immediately recognized a few names - Penlight, the forest beyond their village, and the towns centered around it.

It was a map. And not just any map, but the most detailed, ornate, and hefty piece of parchment that Jasper had ever seen.

As the young wolf gawked, his mother came over from the stove and placed her hands on her husband's shoulders. "We know you love adventuring, and we know that it's only a matter of time before your adventures span far beyond just our forest here. You take after your father, after all. So we want you to be prepared."

Titan nodded and chuckled a little at that, before gesturing to the map once more and continuing to speak. "The Carnell family has guarded this map since before the days of Penlight, and added to it through their adventures and work within the kingdom – as knights and other servants of the realm – for generations. Upon it are countless territories, and countless treasures - from the old kings' crypts, to even the Abyss Caverns and the long-lost Sun Skewer within them."

With that, Titan extended his hand and the map in it towards Jasper, and bowed his head. "And now... it is your turn to hold the map. To wander wide and far, and to keep the Carnell legacy alive."

Jasper took the map, but was only able to hold it and behold its glory up close for a few moments before tears fogged up his vision, and he glanced up to see both of his parents coming in from the side to wrap him up in a tight, warm embrace.

"T-thank you, I..." The young wolf sniffled and wiped his nose amongst the hug. "I love you both."

Just at that moment a sizzling started to emanate from the stove, and Jasper's mother unclasped her arms and jumped back to attend to it, with Titan following suit some time after – pulling plates down from the pantry and setting them on the table in front of each of their chairs. "We love you too. Our big, grown up son. But now..."

She smiled and turned around with the pan in hand. "It's breakfast time! Your favorite – steak and herbs!"

Jasper tucked in the very second that food was served - eating as fast as he could in his excitement to further examine the map – and was done within what must have been five minutes, while his parents were not even halfway through.

His mother half-sincerely shook her head as he pushed out of his chair, washed his hands, and plucked it up before looking over to her beseechingly. "Can I..?"

Fantasia tilted her head, prompting her son to continue in an eager, pleading tone. "Just to explore in the forest for a little while! I'll be back for dinner, I promise!"

Titan chuckled around a bite of meat, while Fantasia rolled her eyes but picked back up a warm smile nonetheless. "Absolutely! Although I don't think there's much for you to discover out there after all these years, even with that map!"

"Thanks, Mom!"

Quicker than a flash, Jasper ran to his room, donned a leather jerkin atop his cotton shirt, slung the sword that his father had gone to the blacksmith to pick out with him when he'd been younger to his hip, and dashed past the kitchen table to pluck up the map after giving his – still eating – parents a kiss on the cheek each.

Opening the family house's front door to be greeted by the morning sunlight of the village street outside, Jasper took a deep breath, and made his first steps past the threshold onto cobblestone.

And, just maybe – today, or someday soon – I'll find an adventure! It is my birthday, after all!

The further Michelle ran, the more that Unity's anger devolved into sadness. She was sobbing unconsolably by the time that the trees had risen to fully cover the smoke rising from the ruins of the orphanage and the noises of panic and chaos from its occupants, and her only thoughts were of fleeting shock and regret. *We should have gone back. We could have saved her.*

Why did this happen? Why to me – why to Ms. Harper? Nothing makes sense.

Eventually Michelle began to stagger and huff a little amongst her stride, the dark energy about her fading visibly, and Unity was torn out of her spiraling, repetitive thoughts as she was placed down knee-first against a fallen tree stump.

The impact hurt a little, leaving the cat girl to call out and cradle her leg as Michelle too came to a sharp halt next to her, breathing heavily, but she didn't wait long before pulling herself back to her feet – ignoring a cry of protest from her muscles and pumping heart.

"Your powers are that s-strong? And you didn't use them to save Ms. Harper? I-" The cat girl hissed, stepping forward to tower over Michelle's prone form. "Why did you take us away from there? Why did you leave her to die?"

Although she barely seemed able to stay up sitting, Michelle shook her head and answered in her usual cool tone. "I felt a power in that person. A powerful one. Far more powerful than mine. We couldn't have done anything. Please be calm – at least we're alive."

Turning away from Michelle with a shake of her head, Unity growled and lashed out at a nearby tree with her foot – ignoring the jolt of pain that came as a result amidst her fury. "Calm down? My-" Another kick. "Our home was just destroyed, Ms. Harper just…"

I'll kill her. I will find who did this, and take revenge.

That was when her anger boiled over, and the first sob escaped from the cat girl's lips. Reaching up to clutch at her face with a mixture of rage and grief, Unity tried to rub the tears back in, but they kept flowing nonetheless – dripping about the fur of her cheeks and wrists.

A few seconds later, she felt a hand on her shoulder and hesitated mid-heave to glance back at Michelle, who was standing just behind her with a more sympathetic, understanding tint to her cool expression than usual. "We have to keep moving. That woman could be anywhere, and we can't die for nothing, when Ms. Harper sacrificed herself just to let us flee."

For a long moment Unity tried and struggled to regulate her breathing, before she finally huffed, shrugged Michelle's hand off, and huffed. "Fine."

With no concept of direction aside from moving 'away from the orphanage, the two began to walk side by side – navigating between seemingly identical tree after tree while Unity continued to stew in her thoughts and incredulity about what had just happened. *I can't believe this happened. Everything gone. Everything. Ms. Harper…*

Let it out. It will only be a matter of time before you don't have any choice in the matter anyway. You are alone, and helpless. Neither of you know where you're going. This will end very soon.

The voice again. The cat girl gritted her teeth. *Shut up!*

Before the voice could taunt her any further, however, her autopilot was snapped off and her tracks were cut short by Michelle holding out her arm in front of her.

Unity glanced around urgently – dropping her frustrated scowl in favor of scanning the trees and bushes surrounding them. "Is it..?"

The snake shook her head dismissively, although her eyes remained darting to and fro as well. "No. I cannot sense any powers. But I heard something."

The two paused there upon the forest ground for a long moment, ears trained to catch any further unusual spikes of noise among the twittering of the birds and the shifting of branches in the wind.

Yet, after what felt like a minute, nothing came.

Both girls straightened up, looked to one another, and prepared to set themselves back on their way, although neither of them was more sure about where they were headed than before.

At that moment, however, an entirely unexpected voice came from behind them – youthful, bright, and quite loud.

"Hey there! What are you doing all the way out here?"

The two girls whirled about where they stood to see a bright-eyed, scruffy, gray-furred wolf boy with a sword strapped to his side and a large piece of parchment in both of his hands stood just between two nearby trees.

Unity gasped, and Michelle raised her hand to summon dark pools of magic – causing the young new arrival to wrap up his map and stow it away before raising both hands diplomatically. "Woah! I mean no harm, I'm sorry!"

Both the snake and the cat girl watched the wolf boy's movements closely for a few moments, before Michelle finally lowered her hands – prompting the wolf boy himself to step forward and tilt his head curiously. "My name is Jasper! Haven't seen either of you around here before."

Michelle answered before Unity could snap out anything bitter. "My name is Michelle, and this is Unity."

Jasper beamed wider than any smile Unity had ever seen anyone else give. "Great to meet you! And what are you doing in the forest?"

"None of your-"

Unity's companion beat her to it again, cutting the cat girl's defensive remark short. "Lost. We're lost."

While Unity clenched her fists by her sides and stewed at having been interrupted and the wolf boy's chipper demeanor, the snake pointed to a long, leather cylinder tucked into the side of his jerkin with a long, scaled finger. "What's that?"

The young stranger first glanced down, and then back up to Michelle with powerful enthusiasm written across his face. "My family's map! We've maintained it for generations. I've been studying it and using it to navigate the forest all morning! Today's my birthday, and my father gave it to me as a gift!"

Unity raised her eyebrow at that, bitter demeanor dimming a little. *So he can be useful after all.* "So you can show us the way out of the forest, right?"

Enthusiasm peaking yet higher, Jasper nodded. "That's nothing! This map has the entire kingdom on it, and much more! Castles, villages... even treasure like the Sun Skewer!"

At first the cat girl was tempted to scoff out loud and roll her eyes at the wolf boy's prattling, but she restricted herself to simply shrugging. "Lead the way, then. Out of here."

Jasper seemed a little shocked by her shortness at first, but soon nodded and turned about to start walking out of the glade and into the depths of the forest again. "A-alright. Follow me!"

For a good fifteen minutes, Unity and Michelle kept pace with the wolf boy as he wove them between small, almost indistinguishable landmarks and narrow brooks – occasionally glancing down to the map in his hands as he did so.

Just as they settled back into the rhythm of walking, however, and Unity had begun to drown out her intrusive thoughts, Jasper began to hum – following a seemingly random melody up and down as they made between tree after tree. *I can't believe this – our only chance at making it out of here before this monster finds us, and he's making going back to the orphanage seem tempting.*

Before the noise could drive her so far as to bring Unity to snap, however, they came to another small clearing along the side of a narrow river, and Michelle stopped in her tracks once more – just like she had earlier, before they had run into Jasper. "Stop. Someone's close again. And this time..."

Jasper stood too, and his ears perked up. "You're right, someone's coming."

The trees shifted with a loudness that even Unity perceived, and the cat girl's chest tightened as an all-too-familiar dark, robed figure stepped out of the forest.

The mystery woman who had destroyed the orphanage.

As the trio bristled uncertainly, and Michelle extended both palms to her sides like she had when they had faced off against King, the figure came to stand in the center of the small clearing. Although her face and form remained imperceptible behind the darkness of her hooded robe, the gloating tone in her voice was clear even before she spoke.

"There you are. I knew that you wouldn't get far."

It didn't take long for Unity's earlier anger to surge back after her initial surprise faded. "You..." She took first one step forward, and then began to run towards the figure with a roared yell building in her throat. "You killed Ms. Harper!"

"Unity, no!"

Just like she had earlier back at the orphanage, Unity felt an incorporeal yank at her shoulders, and was tugged back from rushing towards the figure.

At first the cat girl growled and wheeled about on Michelle to scold her for her interference, but when she did so, she found the snake girl panting a little and waving her hands. "My magic... I'm too tired for now..."

The figure remained entirely still throughout all of this, and only moved her head once Unity came back to behold her with a growl – tilting her hood as though looking the two girls up and down. "There's the strength I felt. The strength that brought me here."

She took a deep, slow breath, as Unity continued to pant and huff with fury. "Finding you had its costs, yes... this Ms. Harper among them... but this moment is worth a thousand times more."

Next, the figure extended one long, gloved hand. "There is no use making this more painful than necessary. Come. We have a long way ahead of us, and only you can serve as my guide."

Unity opened her mouth to snap something back, and readied her legs to spring up and attack again despite Michelle's warning and restraint, but Jasper beat her to it – stepping in front of both girls with the sword that had been at his side raised in the air. "Stay away from them! I don't know who you are, or what you want, but they're not coming with you!"

The figure sighed, and turned her head to the trees to her side. "Maple?"

There was yet another rustle in the nearby bushes, and like clockwork, a cloth and leather-wearing human with long, thin hair, scars across his face, and an untrimmed stubble below them stepped out to advance upon the trio – reaching back to take a glinting steel axe from his side as he moved.

Jasper unsheathed his sword and stepped forward in front of Unity and Michelle with a wordless, slightly shaky cry, but it only took a few feints and half-blows from the newly-arrived human to knock the wolf-boy off balance, and send him landing hard on his back on the grass with a dull thud.

Before Maple could follow up and strike his fallen 'opponent' again, however, Maple's hooded companion raised her arm, and step forward. "Let me finish this. Mercifully. He's just a child, after all."

Maple bowed back, lowering his axe, and the figure advanced in turn – stepping nearer to Jasper, who attempted to scramble back on the ground, but only succeeded in backing himself up against the trunk of a tree.

Unity's heart jumped into her throat at the sight, and she could feel even Michelle tensing by her side. They'd just barely learned the wolf boy's name, but the thought that they could be about to see him die right here and now – after all the terrible loss the day had already brought – was terrifying.

The figure slowly extended her arm, and from its palm a long, slender blade of golden magic began to extend - just like that the figure had used to end Ms. Harper – longer and longer until it had almost reached Jasper's side, and...

Stopped just short - where, poking out of his jerkin, the leather wrapping of the wolf's family map was visible.

"Now... what's this? Is that..." The hooded figure's head snapped back, almost as though in realization, before her gloved hand stretched forward. "Give it to me, child. Now."

Scrambling away on his back, Jasper reached down to tuck the map further into his jerkin. "No! T-that's mine!"

Golden energy began to crackle up the figure's arms. "What did I say about making this more painful than necessary?"

Letting out an exerted huff, Michelle reached forward with her arms in response to the figure's apparent readiness to strike. "Jasper! Let it go!"

Whining sharply through both anxiety and clear reluctance, Jasper ever so slowly reached to his side, produced the wrapped map, and handed it outwards to the figure, who snatched it up with a triumphant hiss, and began to unravel it roughly as the wolf boy could only watch on in horror.

Once the figure had the map spread out in her arms, her hood turned to and fro, scanning to and fro across its surface. "The Sun Skewer... I don't know how... but it's here. It doesn't matter now. It's time. It's finally, finally time."

At first Maple, who had been standing to the side with his axe over his shoulder watching the scene unfold, blinked in bewilderment at his companion's actions, but then he shrugged and turned back to slowly advance on the children before him as Jasper pulled himself to his feet up against the tree and hefted his sword with a low growl. "Change of plans, then."

Unity, however, had other ideas. Taking advantage of a split second moment in which the human was focused on Jasper instead of herself and Michelle, the cat girl lashed out with her leg at an angle – knocking Maple off his feet to land on the root-studded forest ground.

As the man groaned and cradled the site of impact, Unity tensed – expecting the hooded figure to react or lash out at them with some form of attack. Yet she remained completely still - the gaze beneath her hood locked on the map in her hands as the three teenagers regained their footing properly, and Unity glanced over to her companions with urgency.

"Run!"

Moving first, Jasper sheathed his sword, hefted his hands up to his body, and began to bolt between the trees at full speed, leaving Michelle and Unity to scramble after in a desperate effort to keep up.

Though the natural buzz of forest life continued all around her, and she could feel the warmth of the sun upon her cloaks, Glimmer paid all of it no mind. No – for her senses were focused on something much, much more important. A trace on the wind. A trace that followed the lines upon the map in front of her. She could sense the magic with every bone in her body - almost literally taste it on the tip of her tongue. So close, yet so far.

The map's lines looked so mundane, so *usual* to the naked eye. But the longer Glimmer stared, the more she saw. The more she understood. The more she smiled. *Fate was kind to me today. Not only the girl... but a perfect replacement. Now, instead of sniffing the ground for magic, it will reveal itself to me as plainly as the day.*

My waiting is over. I'm coming, oh-so-elusive Sun Skewer. I'm coming, revenge.

"My lady?"

Glimmer's head snapped to the side to regard the man standing beside her – still covered in some leaves and twigs after the two girls had pushed him over earlier. He was dull, for all his sharpness with a blade, but he was also a dutiful servant. One of many that she had at her disposal, thanks to her years of planning. And would make full use of across the coming journey.

There was no holding back now. Not when her plan was so close to success, and all the pieces were falling into line.

Glimmer's eyes fell back to the map in her hands, and she smiled again. *So neat, and so obedient. Just like they are, and just like she will be, with time.*

"Should we follow them, my lady?"

The shrouded woman arched an eyebrow beneath her cloaks at the return of her servant's voice. "We? No, Maple. I can't afford to waste more time here. Not when I have a key after all, at least."

Next, she leveled her masked head back towards Maple. "Capture her, and bring her to me as I travel. Having her would be useful, yes, but so long as I can find the Skewer, I can begin."

Maple nodded, but then his obedient expression shifted somewhat towards uncertainty. "And if I can't find her? The forest is large, my lady, and Penlight is even larger. I lack your magical senses to track her down."

Glimmer waved her hand dismissively. "She will prove easier to find than you might think. I am beyond sure that curiosity will drive her to me regardless. Whether you find her, or she finds you - we haven't seen the last of her just yet."

"I understand. But what about the others?"

The cloaked woman turned away from him – already starting to pace away across the forest ground with a swish of her cloak.

"Kill them. No use in leaving meddlers stray - or loose threads, for that matter."

4

Hearts beating hard, breaths coming in rough gasps, and feet thudding upon the forest ground in an unsteady, urgent rhythm, Unity and Michelle ran after Jasper as the wolf boy wove his way between trees and hills – barely able to keep up with his energetic stride.

Eventually, Unity mustered the composure to shout out mid-stride. "Jasper! Where are we going?"

Jasper's response trailed back to them, though he neglected to turn back. "I know just where we can hide, don't worry! I know these forests like the back of my hand."

The cat girl frowned despite her lingering panic and shock. *Can we trust him? If we're just running in circles, that woman could find us. And then... maybe we won't be so lucky.*

But it's not like we have any other option right now.

After what felt like an eternity, and with the sun dulling to deep orange in the sky, the trees parted a little, and the trio made their way out of the forest onto what appeared to be a path cutting through its middle. It was only now that Jasper slowed somewhat – coming to a light trot along the cobblestone road, and finally allowing the two girls behind him to catch up in a huff of desperate breath-catching.

Before they could ask him where they were headed, however, the trees ahead thinned out yet further, and Unity squinted to see the thatch and tile roofs of a small collection of houses beyond them. "A... town?"

The wolf turned to glance over his shoulder with a smile – seeming not at all exhausted or fazed by their flight. "*My* town! My home is just over there!" He lifted one hand, pointing towards one of the closest buildings – a humble yet cozy-looking house with a hedge about the outside and flower baskets below the windows.

A few moments later they were standing in front of the house's door, Jasper knocked upon it, and Unity glanced to and fro up the street as they waited for someone to answer. Most of the buildings here along the tree-lined road were similar in common style and furnishing, but amongst them, there was a single structure that stuck out – overgrown, with broken windows and a moss-furred path.

It looked... almost sad, although the cat girl couldn't quite grasp why. *Maybe it was well cared-after, once. Loved. And yet now it's abandoned. Just like I was.*

But then the threshold in front of them practically slammed open, and Unity's head jerked back around to see a tall, beaming wolf woman dressed in a lavender blouse and trousers standing over them.

"Jasper! You're home early! Did you forget something for the forest?" Her kindly eyes widened, and ranged over Michelle and Unity in turn. "And who are these two young ladies?"

Unity's mouth drifted open uncertainty as she tried to think up an answer, but Jasper beat her to it. "Unity and Michelle! I found them in the forest."

That caused the woman's smile to fade a little, and her head to quirk in open curiosity. "Is that so? Where are your parents?"

Michelle replied now, her voice as flat as ever. "We're orphans."

Jasper's mother's confusion deepened further. "From the orphanage? I'm afraid I don't quite understand."

Unity could only nod, not exactly feeling up to telling the truth. "Yes. We're just... taking a day out. Jasper invited us over for a, uh..."

"Sleepover!" The young wolf piped up to cut Unity's hesitation short. *So he's playing along.*

The moment of awkwardness passed, and Jasper's mother's earlier enthusiasm returned in full force. "Well, then! Any friend of Jasper's is a warmly welcome guest in the Carnell household!"

The wolf woman stepped back from the door and ushered them inside. "Please – do come inside, all of you! My name is Fantasia! If you'd like, you can go wash up, and then we'll have dinner!"

Jasper darted in on through the plain but charming hallway beyond without another word, and Unity and Michelle followed not long behind – although they moved a little more cautiously.

How long will we be safe – here or anywhere?

Unity stared into the Carnells' round bathroom mirror, and the tired, dark-eyed cat-girl reflected there stared back. The soot and streaks of dried blood that had caked her fur had been washed away, but the debris and damage within her mind was far more reluctant to fade.

Your powers are that strong, and you didn't use them to save Ms. Harper? And we had so much faith in you...

It was almost impossible to tell the voices from her own dark, cyclical thoughts by now. The visions of Ms. Harper's body. The explosion. The fires, and the screaming. How... normal and calm everything felt now, within this haven of a house, and amongst this almost sickly-sweet family.

The cat-girl cursed and pushed away from the basin, giving one last wipe with the back of her hand to dry her face. *Not like this is the worst thing that's happened to me. Damn that place. Damn this house. Damn everything.*

A few moments later she'd made her way out into the hall and from there into the dining hall, where Michelle, Jasper, his mother, and a larger male who was clearly Jasper's father by terms of resemblance were sat about the laid table, and the house's window showed that the sun had set completely outside. An awfully domestic scene, in contrast to the wilderness and even the orphanage they had left behind.

Which, as she was welcomed by all present and sat down at the table, was something that struck the cat girl powerfully in its unfamiliarity, and almost brought a tear to her eye.

Jasper treats this as though it's so... normal. And yet... it's like nothing I've ever seen, or dared dream for.

Jasper's father, Titan, was a portly, strong-looking man with an even more powerful laugh, and proved to be so rowdy during dinner that even his wife had to *tut* him back to a milder tone every so often. Yet, despite this, both the atmosphere and the food itself – a stew of some kind with varying vegetables – were almost enough to dull the edge of Unity's anxiety and shock altogether. Or, at least, help her forget them for a moment.

But by the time that the meal had come to a close, and Titan set about clearing the table, she could feel an edge of uncertainty returning within her – which was not exactly helped by Fantasia standing and directly regarding both her and Michelle with a warm smile. "Do come with me, girls! I'll show you your room for the night."

A moment or two later, the two were ushered into a room down the hall where Unity had visited the bathroom, with Jasper just behind them. Inside, there were a stack of boxes against one wall, a desk with a candle atop it on the other, and a set of two sleeping rolls laid out on the wooden floor in the center.

Fantasia stood in the doorway, looking quite sheepish for the first time since welcoming them in. "You two can rest in here for the night. I'm sorry for the lack of proper sleeping arrangements, but it's the very best we could find at such short notice." She nodded eagerly, and her smile returned in full force. "But if you need anything else just let me know, alright?"

Making her way into the center of the room and looking from Fantasia to the rolls and back while Michelle and Jasper moved over to stand near the desk, Unity gave her best attempt at a smile of her own. "Thanks. We... really appreciate you letting us stay here."

The wolf woman shook her head. "Oh, it's nothing. As I said – a friend of Jasper's is a friend of the Carnell family! Truly, just ask if you need anything!"

Fantasia closed the door behind her with one last warm wave, leaving the room entirely dark except for the small candle on the desk.

Jasper, whose tail was wagging with clear anticipation, failed to wait long at all before springing the question he'd clearly been dying to ask. "So. I don't want to pry, but... why were those two chasing you?"

Unity's mouth dried up at the memory as she tried to form an explanation. "We were..."

After she trailed into silence, Michelle filled in instead – although her eyes were preoccupied watching the candle on the desk. "They attacked our orphanage. Looking for someone. And we escaped."

Unity's thoughts said what she could not. *Thanks to you. The voices really wanted me to go back – who knows what might have happened?*

Jasper seemed horrified. "An attack? In Penlight? The Knights have to know about it. At least, I hope so." His head tilted, just as it had earlier in the day when they'd met him. "Do you know why or what they wanted?"

"No idea – but that woman seemed to think Ms. Harper would know. And earlier today, she mentioned something about the 'Sun Skewer.'"

"My dad mentioned that this morning! It was on my family's map." Jasper tilted his head to the side at that. "But who's Ms. Harper?"

Unity's mouth opened, but her throat choked, and she sat there silent for a moment before anything came out. "She's... she was..."

Michelle cut in – voice as uninflected as ever. "The head of the orphanage. The strange woman killed her."

"Oh, that's..." Jasper's expression drooped at first, but then perked back up in urgency. "Well, if they're looking for you, do you think they'll come here?" He shook his head. "We can't stay anyway - we have to get that map back. It was my Dad's! My entire family's! I can't tell them I lost it, and besides – you expect me to turn down an adventure?"

At first Unity wanted to roll her eyes at the wolf's ever-present tone of excitement, but then a wave of motivation rolled over her instead, and her expression darkened. "And I'm not letting her get away with killing Ms. Harper. Whatever she wants the map for... we're not letting her have it."

Jasper's head tilted again. "But how are we supposed to find her without the map?"

"I know how."

The two turned to Michelle, who had her gaze directed to the floorboards beneath them. "I can sense her power from a distance, after feeling it today. Her power, and..." The snake's eyes lifted to Unity's. "All magic."

A moment of silence passed between the three, before Michelle broke the tense atmosphere by addressing Jasper instead. "But what will you tell your parents?"

The wolf simply shrugged. "To not worry. I've camped in the forest for ages before. As long as I come back some time soon, they trust me to look out for myself. Today's my sixteenth birthday, after all!"

Even Unity found that a little relieving. *That's something I don't have to worry about either, at least. Guess having this dork around for muscle won't be a pure burden after all.*

The conversation had clearly come to a halt, however, and the cat girl's patience was wearing thin – especially with the noise and storm of emotions swirling within her head. As such, before either of the others could speak up once more, Unity stood and stretched her arms. "Anyway, we need to sleep. It's been... a long day."

Jasper blinked for a moment before standing too, nodding sheepishly. "Oh! Yeah, sure, I'll let you two get some rest. We can head out in the morning!"

The wolf boy backed up - opening, stepping past, and closing the door through which his mother had left minutes before. A beam of light from the hall outside entered the room while the threshold was open, but then it vanished, and Unity and Michelle were left alone once more – glancing over to one another silently for a second, before going about making their sleeping rolls as comfortable as they could without exchanging words.

Once they were done, Unity reached over to snuff out the candle on the table, and pressed herself flat onto the roll with closed eyes. Everything was so familiar that she could literally feel it eating at her brain – this 'bed', the room's smell, the shuffles of noises in other parts of the house. Everything.

"Good night, Unity."

At first Unity scowled at the snake girl's gesture. *She really thinks we're best friends now, just because of what happened?*

But then the thought and the weight of 'what happened' hit her again, harder than ever, and she had to squeeze her eyes shut in the dark to stop tears from prickling in their corners. Michelle was all she had from the old world now – as loathe as she was to admit it. Even King and his thugs were gone forever, most likely. She *was* her friend. And without her...

Not only would she have nothing left at all, but she would have no idea how or why to keep going.

"Good night, Michelle."

5

— · —

Clashes of metal against metal and the sound of booming bursts of magic rang through Penlight Castle's training yard – heralding, more often than not, a particularly energetic, or even reckless, strike from one of the two girls sparring in its center.

The first of the two, with brown fur, short red hair, and a navy blue jacket over her shoulders, was Amethyst – holding a spear between two clenched sets of knuckles. Her opponent, who bore a short sword in one hand and a crackling orb of energy in her other, was none other than Justice. Amethyst's sister had her piercing blue eyes and her flame-colored hair, but the latter was far longer, and she wore a simple white cotton blouse that whipped to and fro about her blonde fur between each strike they traded.

As the two clashed, however, trading blows both magic and physical in nature, a third figure watched from the edge of the courtyard – analyzing their every move with not only the caring eye of a father, but also deep responsibility. They were doing well, yes, but would it be enough?

Kijury sighed, and furrowed his brow. They were still young, and yet upon their shoulders, as upon the shoulders of all Penlight's knights and protectors, rested the fate of the kingdom, and its magic.

One particularly wild blast of energy sent out a shockwave of air that Kijury could feel from across the yard, and was enough to bring the deer to raise his arm and call out. "Stop. That's enough."

Moving to obey instantly, Justice dropped out of her fighting stance mid-cast, and her sister wasn't long behind. Before long, the two girls were standing to attention next to one another – panting slightly, but overall looking beyond satisfied with their performance over the last ten minutes.

Justice looked over at her sister with an exhausted smile. "Ugh... you're so quick."

Amethyst smiled in return and shrugged. "Quicker than you, at least."

The two seemed poised for further friendly bickering, but before they could do so, a fourth voice rang out from behind Kijury.

"Excellent work, girls. You're improving every day."

The deer and his daughters turned about on the spot to see a tall, black leather-clad figure with familiar flame-colored hair striding across the training pitch towards them, bearing a smile upon her face. "And this is only the beginning. Soon you will master magic as well - and alongside it, the protective might of a ruler."

Amethyst beamed especially wide at her mother's words. "I can't wait, mother."

Growing nearer, Destiny bowed her head. "I'm sure, my dear."

Before Kijury or the girls could say more, however, the Queen raised her arm to the sinking sun, which had touched the horizon beyond the training yard's walls. "But that is enough for the day. You've been out here training since the morning, and I'm sure you're all hungry."

"Aye, that we are." Kijury gave a smile of his own and stepped towards his wife – holding out his arm so that Justice and Amethyst could join them in walking towards the training yard's exit.

Later that day, after lunch had been enjoyed and the afternoon had properly arrived, Destiny called Justice aside from the table where her father and sister were discussing Penlight military victories of old with a gentle upwards jerk of the head.

Justice answered by obediently pulling out of her chair and making over to the side of the room, although with her head already tilted to the side with curiosity.

"You and your sister did excellently, earlier today."

Justice beamed. "Thank you, mother."

The Queen tilted her head. "Although, at the same time..."

That made the young deer-canine frown. "Although?"

Destiny offered her a reassuring smile, and took Justice's hand. "Come with me, please."

The two walked together through the halls of the castle for a minute – passing doorway after doorway and the occasional servant or knight until they arrived at the hold's entry hall, where the Queen's throne sat, and the far wall was lined with two score of portraits.

The Queen led her daughter to the rightmost of these portraits, and gestured to it with the hand not currently clasping Justice's. "This is King Aldrich. He was the one who trusted me with the throne. Trusted magic to protect the kingdom."

She sighed deeply, and gently pulled her daughter in – bringing them so that she could look down into Justice's sharp blue eyes. "And, one day, you will be the one trusted with both magic and to protect the kingdom."

Justice nodded eagerly. "I know, mother. I can do it."

Destiny bowed her head, seeming more solemn than ever. "I know you can. I just don't want all this weight... to fall upon you too suddenly. Either of you. You both deserve all the time to find yourselves and your strengths that I and the kingdom are able to afford you."

The Queen released Justice's hand, paused for a moment, and took a deep breath - seeming to clear her thoughts.

Before she could continue, however, there was a great creak of wood and metal behind them, and Destiny and Justice both turned to see an opossum dressed in a dark gray cloak and simple leathers making her way through the chamber door towards them at a rapid pace.

Spreading her arms, Destiny nodded in the new arrival's direction. "Umi – I'm glad to see you. But what has you in such a rush?"

The knight bowed her head as she drew near to her queen, but wasted no time with further formalities before raising her deep purple, worry-filled eyes back up to Destiny's. "Something is wrong. I can feel it."

Destiny frowned. "Wrong? In the kingdom? Or do you mean with…"

The Queen trailed off, and Umi nodded.

Before she could say more, however, the door behind them opened yet again, and another figure strode through – a human with long, flowing blonde hair, and garb almost identical to Umi's. Ika Raiden.

Ika skipped formalities altogether in her approach, and raised her voice with sharp urgency. "There was an attack, my lady. Or an accident – we can't tell just yet."

Destiny's already dire expression tightened further. "By Ophin. Where? And by whom?"

Ika shook her head, breathing heavily and clearly worn out from her speedy approach. "Penlight Orphanage. And we have no information, my lady, I'm sorry."

The Queen's demeanor became severe, and she turned to glance over her shoulder in her daughter's direction, where she was watching the scene unfold with her jaw hanging slightly open. "Go to your father and sister. Wait for my return."

Mouth snapping shut, Justice bowed obediently, and made to leave the chamber without a second's delay. "Yes, mother."

A few frantic minutes of travel through the streets of Penlight and then the castle's outskirts later, Destiny, Umi, and the queen's contingent of guards arrived at the long, winding road that approached the Orphanage. But where the pair expected to find the building's grand, ornate shape upon crossing the last tree line, their eyes were instead met with…

Nothing. Clean, orange afternoon sky, all the way down to below the height of the trees themselves, where they finally could see what had once been the Orphanage – now little more than a pile of blackened, mixed shards of stone and wood with guardsmen patrolling around them, searching for survivors.

Both Destiny and Umi let out a loud gasp of shock as they approached properly, and the full scale of the wreckage revealed itself to them. There was, simply, next to nothing left, and even their first cursory glance about the clearing revealed more than a few clearly injured children and servants, who were either being helped up or attended to by the twenty-odd Penlight guardsmen that dotted the area.

After a few seconds of shock, Destiny's eyes caught a familiar face amongst the flock of soldiers – or, rather, the absence of one. Yuuto Touma.

Raising her arm, she called out sharply. "Yuuto. Have you discovered what happened yet?"

After catching sight of his queen and immediately pacing over, the horn-masked man gave a short bow – his answer hushed. "Magic, my lady. The guardsmen are none the wiser, but I can sense it everywhere."

That brought a look of dark realization to Destiny's face. "I can too. And not just any kind of magic, either." She returned to scanning the clearing, but not without first glancing back at Umi to see an equally terrified expression upon the opossum's face. "Please tell me you've found-"

Yuuto shook his head. "Not a single sign, my lady. But, on the other hand, we're growing close to confident that we've accounted for all the other children - alive or otherwise. And only she and one other are still missing."

Umi let out an audible huff of concern at that. But then she took a deep breath, steadied herself, and turned to face Destiny, who was watching her with great concern in her piercing eyes. "No. She is alive, I know it. Out there... somewhere."

The queen nodded. "I know it too. She will find safety."

"Unity is bound to be strong – just like her mothers."

6

— • —

The morning light came far faster than Unity had thought it would. Faster than she'd hoped, in a way, leaving her with little time to collect her thoughts.

It had been beyond strange, sleeping in her sundress, and somewhere other than her dormitory in the orphanage for the first time in memory, but she'd steeled herself through it – and kept herself from crying – by drowning out the unfamiliarity and any flashbacks to Ms. Haper's lifeless form with thoughts of determination and revenge.

By the time Unity woke up and went to wash her face in the bathroom - her back a little sore from the thinness of the bedrolls – Michelle, Jasper, and his mother seemed to have been awake for hours, and looked up from their seats at kitchen table when the cat girl entered with almost identical smiles on the wolves' part.

Fantasia was the first to speak – beckoning Unity forward to take up the last available seat while she mixed a bowl of what appeared to be fruit cereal in her hands. "Jasper told me that you three are going out into the forest again today! He does love his adventures – and it would seem you do too! Titan told me to pass on his wishes – he had to go to his shift at the castle already."

The cat girl followed the gesture, and lowered herself down into the creaking seat with a hesitant glance over at Jasper, who smiled back and gave her a cheesy thumbs up. *So he can lie.* "Uh, yeah. Just to get out a bit."

Now the wolf woman turned to her son with a more motherly tone. "And, Jasper, do you have your bag, the map, and everything else you need, hmm?"

The younger wolf scoffed and mock-rolled his eyes. "I'm sixteen, Mom. I can care for myself."

Unity stopped herself from quirking her eyebrow. *We don't have the map. He's willing to lie?*

Fantasia paused in her stirring for a moment, seeming almost wistful, before nodding and continuing her earlier motions. "You're right. But please do take care, my son."

A bowl of breakfast for each of them later, Jasper stood up from the table, donned his leather jerkin, slung a satchel from under his chair over his back, and pulled his sword out from within it to strap it to his side as Michelle and Unity watched on – with the cat girl feeling direly unequipped by comparison. *No home, no food, no money... Nothing but the skin and fur on our backs.*

Fantasia took her time sending them off and wishing them well, but before they knew it, they had stepped out past the Carnell house's threshold, and were staring down the village's morning-lit street with the weight of what they were thinking to undertake hanging heavy on their shoulders.

Jasper had seemed completely unbothered through the entire morning, and neglected to even turn back to wave to his mother watching them make away through the house's window, and Michelle had clearly taken note of that fact – approaching the wolf boy from behind and tapping him on the shoulder before they'd taken more than a few steps. "Are you okay with this? We didn't exactly tell the whole truth."

Unity could have almost sighed aloud, but silenced herself by working her hands in the fabric of her dress instead. *We need him. For his memory of the map, if nothing else. Don't make him back out now.*

Yet Jasper only shrugged as they moved further towards the tree line. "Why shouldn't I be? My father was an adventurer – and so will I be! The earlier, the better!"

That seemed to be a good enough answer for Michelle – and with that, their feet left the cobblestone of the village road, and took them back into the arms and foliage of the forest and its tweeting birds.

Nothing of note happened for quite some time afterwards, and the trio shared no words – leaving Unity feeling a little disappointed, if anything, in the wake of the tension that had been building up within her all night at the thought of setting out.

The silence left her time to think about other things, however. Yesterday. The future. And, most strikingly... the voices in her head.

Acting completely on irrational impulse, Unity sped up as they passed beneath a particularly low tree to swoop up and tap Michelle's shoulder just as the gray snake girl had tapped Jasper's earlier. "Michelle. I..."

The snake looked back and tilted her head as she walked, before replying at full volume. "Why are you whispering?"

Jasper glanced over his shoulder in confusion at the snake's sudden raised tone, causing Unity to scowl and turn to Michelle with a sharp *sssh*. "Keep your voice down. I have something to tell you. Only you."

The snake looked almost as confused as Jasper had, but eventually nodded, and Unity continued – trying to hold both herself and Michelle back from Jasper's oblivious, faster pace up ahead.

"Ever since you arrived, and even more now since... what happened..." She shrugged, still feeling incredibly foolish about what she was about to say. "I've been hearing voices. They tell me to do things. And... warn me of things."

They continued walking in silence for a few seconds, and Unity was hit by a belated realization of how crazy she sounded. *Sound, and probably am. It's the truth, after all.*

But then Michelle, with her eyes still facing forward as they moved, spoke up. "I told you that I can sense magic."

Unity frowned. "Yes, and?"

"I sense it in you." The snake girl's voice was as matter of fact as always. "Maybe you can discover more about it along this journey. Or I can help you."

The cat girl could only blink in surprise. *She can't be serious, right? If I had magic, I'd have known by now, wouldn't I have?* "Do you mean... I have abilities like you do?"

Michelle shrugged, and finally slowed down to turn about and face Unity. "Maybe not like me. I don't know. I've never felt anything like the energy you have before. But there is something."

For a moment Unity hesitated and mulled the revelation of Michelle's words over in her head, but before she could say more, they both heard Jasper's voice from just up ahead amongst the trees. "What are you guys waiting for? We're not going to catch up to that villain by standing here!"

Michelle and Unity scurried to catch up, and found the wolf boy standing with one hand on the hilt of his sword and his usual wide smile across his face.

Once they were reunited and began to move as one, Michelle added one last quip of her own. "Or her servant. Remember, we might not be safe even here."

Before Unity or Jasper could respond, however, there was the sound of a dull thud from behind them, and the trio wheeled about just in time to catch a long-haired human silhouette dropping down from the branches of the trees they had just walked beneath.

It was the axe-bearing warrior Maple who had accompanied Glimmer the day before – covered partially in leaves, and already bearing the shaft of his axe ready in his hand.

Now steady on his feet in the grass and moss, the human shook his head. "I am no servant. But you are right to fear. And I must warn you – you are expendable, now. Lady Glimmer has the map. Come with me – or I am free to deal with you as I see fit."

So that's her name. Unity made note of the information, before stepping forward and jerking her chin upwards with the same obstinance she'd learned to display over long years of conflict with King and his friends. Her heart was racing from the sudden ambush, but she dared not let her surprise show. "Apparently it's you who is expendable. All alone in a forest. Shouldn't you be scared?"

Maple's eyebrows raised at that, though he soon played it off with a scoff and by waving his axe in the air. "You are weak children. You will obey, or I will end you – choose wisely."

Unity's blood boiled at those words. *How dare he.* She growled a little and hefted her fists – prompting Jasper to draw his sword, Michelle to settle into a fighting stance, and lastly Maple to heft his axe as well. "Stupid children, at that. Come, then."

Michelle breathed out deeply, and a dark force began to form between her hands – shimmering, intangible, and now familiar from yesterday.

She has her magic back. The cat girl's thoughts wandered involuntarily. *Just like I could have. Do have, apparently. Could it really be true?*

But then Maple lunged forward amongst the trees, and all was movement and attention-consuming chaos. Jasper fended off the human's first powerful downwards strike – redirecting its momentum to the side with a smoothness that was either luck or more skill than Unity had thought him to have after yesterday's spectacle – but was soon caught by a backhand blow from Maple's leather-padded elbow.

That was when Michelle stepped in – letting out sharp blasts of energy from her palms that caught Maple off guard and disrupted his next blow – leaving him open to an upswing from Jasper, which caught the human in the side.

Just like that, Maple cried out as the young wolf's blade cut through the leather of his jerkin, and fumbled his axe so that it thudded to the ground beside him as he tripped to his knees.

At first the human immediately tried to scramble back up and move for his weapon, but Jasper was quicker – levelling the point of his sword to Maple's throat, even as his hand shook a little, and his expression became visibly upset.

Realizing his predicament, Maple's expression went through shock, desperation, and anger in quick succession, before he spat over his shoulder and looked up with burning, indignant eyes. "Glimmer will end you. She will find the Sun Skewer, as is her right, and she will take what is hers. I will not stop, before I see this through."

Moving forward with both hands spread out to her side, Michelle shook her serpentine head. "Then we have no choice."

Before the human could say more, the snake's hands blasted forth magic once more, and Maple was sent flying off his knees to crash against a nearby tree – after which he slumped lifelessly to the ground.

Both Unity and Jasper's hearts stopped beating for a moment after the impact – both unwilling to go check to see whether their assailant was truly dead. After some time, however, the cat girl knelt and picked up Maple's fallen weapon – tossing it in her hand to test its weight. *Now I have a way to fight back too.*

"Did we really have to..?"

Unity cut Jasper off without even looking up. "Yes."

"But..."

That caused Unity to growl and raise her non-axe-bearing arm in the frightened wolf boy's direction. "No 'but'. Either get used to this, or go back home. We don't have time to worry about things like this when this Glimmer is already moving. If she did what she did to our orphanage just to get to us, who knows what her actual plans are, hunting something like the Sun Skewer."

Jasper stayed silent and blinking for a few moments, before giving Maple's body one last glance, before sighing and turning away to face into the forest ahead of them. "The Sun Skewer?"

Now Michelle piped up – already stepping past Jasper and beginning to weave between trees. "The map, remember? What she said she was looking for. But come – we can't waste any more time on this servant. Glimmer's energy is fading fast, and I have to get a firm grasp to track it."

Heeding Michelle's firm tone, the two left the small clearing in which Maple had ambushed them – leaving the human's crumpled form against the tree where it had landed.

They travelled as swiftly as they could for another half hour – before Unity eventually noticed that the foliage and trees around them were thinning out into dry grassland with each step, and the gritty heaviness the air occasionally bore almost smelled like... desert.

As they came to a particularly patchy spot of grass, Jasper stopped and appeared to think for a long while. "The forest. It ends here."

Unity tilted her head. *Now we just have to hope he remembers at least some of his map.* "Where next?"

The wolf boy craned his neck around to try to glance past the last few trees in front of them, where they petered out altogether. "Some grassland... and then the Arid Frontier, I think."

"Well, what are we waiting for?"

The other two followed Unity's prompting, and took their first few steps beyond the forests' edge – setting out upon the grassland at the hands of Michelle's guidance and Jasper's memory of the map.

For her entire life, the walls of the orphanage and, at most, the trees of the Penlight Forest had seemed like the very borders of Unity's world. Sure, she'd visited the town and castle every so often, but she'd never even dreamt of venturing so far away – leaving not only everything she'd ever known behind, but also Penlight itself.

Yet it doesn't matter now. I'd go just about anywhere to stop that murderer from having her way.

For you, Ms. Harper.

7

— · —

The desert winds outside were wild and merciless, like a void of disorder, but the inside of the tavern was quite serene, and the few patrons of varying species that sat atop the various stools and seats scattered about its interior were calm and composed amongst their drinks and casual conversations.

At least, until the door swung open, and a gust of wind and dust carried through – billowing about the silhouette of a single figure wearing long, dark cloaks.

A few seconds passed, with the patrons of the tavern pausing in their chatter to turn about and stare at the new entry out of curiosity, before they stepped forward and allowed the door to shut behind themselves – plunging the space back into relative darkness.

A few steps later, and the figure was settling down at one of the stools at the tavern's bar – causing them to be soon greeted by the bartender, who was a quite dapper fox with green eyes and a towel wrapped about his arm. "What can I get you… sir?"

The figure waved their hand dismissively, and the bartender gave them a somewhat confused glance before shrugging and turning about to first pour a beverage of some indeterminable sort.

No sooner had he finished pouring than the figure snatched the glass up, turned away from the bar, and approached a table in the corner of the room, where a canid in rough leathers and a wide-brimmed desert hat sat half-concealed by the dark.

Glimmer sat down at the table opposite the hat-bearing man, and set the drink down on the table in front of him. "For being late."

The male *tsk*ed – voice dark and rough. "So kind of you. But my time doesn't come free, as you know."

"It was the first leg on a long journey."

He leaned back in his chair until it rested against the tavern's wall. "And you really think the girl will keep following, if she's attacked?"

Glimmer nodded. "Killing her friends will guarantee it. And her vulnerability, when the time comes."

The canid quirked his head to the side, allowing one sharp, red eye to peek out from beneath the rim of his hat. "She has come this far. Perhaps she is not so vulnerable after all."

"It is true. Maple has already fallen to her – I can sense it. But that is why I am here with you. Who I trust not to fail so unspectacularly as he did."

The male *tsk*ed. "You may think yourself untouchable now that you travel outside of the kingdom, Glimmer. But you of all people should know that the reach of Upholder and her knights is inescapable. Watch your back."

But then, after a moment of silence and a long sip from the drink Glimmer had bought him, the canid shrugged. "All the same – I will play along, and get the attention of this girl. Her friends will die, as you wish."

He clattered the glass to the table, and smiled.

"At my hand, if I get the chance."

"Abandoned. Again."

Poised in the ruined, stony middle of what had perhaps once been a town square, Unity sighed and reached up to dust sand out of the hair and fur of her head. Another settlement that had turned out to be little more than ghost towns made up of dry wood and windowless buildings. *Maybe this wasn't always a desert? Not that it matters now.*

They'd entered the Arid Frontier proper at what had seemed like close to midday, and if her gauging of the sun's height and her sense of time were any measure to go by, Unity was almost certain that they'd spent at least four hours here already. And yet there was no end to the monotony in sight. Dunes, thin, weak trees, and the endless blue sky.

"I'm so hot... would need to shed half of my fur to cool down properly out here."

Unity rolled her eyes and bit back a sigh as they started moving again, and left this latest ruin. *Will he stop complaining?* "It's not that bad. I can barely feel it at all."

This was only half-true, if she'd been honest. Although she seemed to be handling the heat better than Jasper, she could feel fatigue slowly setting in nonetheless. Michelle, however, remained silent and seemed altogether unaffected - which made sense given her species, Unity supposed.

Not that she had given it much thought, all in all. She'd dismissed her qualms and reaction at the time thanks to adrenaline and the urgency of catching up to this Glimmer, but the more time they spent in silence and movement, the more her thoughts lingered on their short but brutal battle with Maple just before leaving the forest.

Sure, her fights over the years with King and his goons had strengthened her stomach to the idea of violence and confrontation, but to actively take someone's life, to have their metaphorical last blood on her hands... was something else.

And yet, deep within her, the source of the voices rejoiced at the thought. She could feel it. It was growing, and, truth be told...

It scared her.

"There's people living here!"

Unity's head jerked upwards, and her tongue stopped working dryly in her mouth in an attempt to summon moisture. Ahead, she found that Jasper's claim had been correct – just beyond the next sandy, rocky outcropping, there was a set of square, wooden buildings that looked to be in far better condition than the others that they had seen that day, and a few figures were visible milling about between them.

A few minutes later, and they were amongst them – avoiding glances from the sparse, dark cloth-dressed crowd as they made down the settlement's single, two-row street until they came to its largest structure – a multi-story building with a single set of swinging doors.

Jasper picked up his pace towards that entrance, and gestured for the others to follow. "That looks like some kind of tavern. Come on – we'll see if anyone has seen Glimmer."

Unity and Michelle moved after him, and soon the trio passed through the tavern's twin swinging doors. Within, they found a medium-sized hall with a sparse few windows on either side wall, and a scattering of tables and patrons drinking and chattering quietly spaced out between the entrance and the bar at the end of the space.

There they found a rugged fox of indeterminate age cleaning a glass, whose ears perked up at the sound of their approach. "Welcome to the Dusty-"

The barkeep interrupted his habitual greeting halfway as he caught a proper glimpse of the trio standing before him. "Well, now. What do you children think's got your business in a place like this?"

Unity scowled. "We're not children. I'm sixteen."

The barkeep raised an eyebrow, but shrugged. "Suit yourself. Ain't nobody here who'll give much of a hoot either way if something goes south." He gestured to the bar. "Can I get ya something? Water, of course."

Unity scowled. "We don't need your help."

"Yes, please. She means yes." Michelle, as usual.

The barkeep chuckled a little and turned around to fetch three glasses – thudding them to the bar before reaching about, producing a tanned sack of fluid, and beginning to pour it into each.

"Fine." Unity rolled her eyes, but snatched one glass up when the barkeep was done and put it to her lips. Soon after the cool liquid began to run down her throat, however, she realized how much she'd needed to drink after their long day of travel.

For a while the three simply sat there at the bar and sipped in silence – resting their bones upon the barstools, and glancing about the room behind them. Eventually, however, Unity's gaze fell on a lanky, leather armor-wearing human man sat alone in the center of the room – holding a full drink in his hand that he didn't seem to have even sipped from, and watching the tavern's door with a gaze like a hawk.

The cat girl turned to the bartender and thumbed over her shoulder. "Who's that?"

The fox took one glance and shook his head. "That's Manto. Knight from the kingdom. And one thing's certain - if Manto is in town, trouble's not far behind." He tilted his head at the young trio once more as Michelle continued to lap away at her water. "In lieu of that, best be keeping to yourself for the evenin'. You three have anywhere to sleep out here?"

A long moment of silence passed, in which none of the three children said anything or moved, before the barkeep scoffed and threw up his hands. "Didn't think so. Well - you can have one of the rooms upstairs for a free night. Ain't nobody else out here at this time of year looking to stay."

Jasper beamed, and nodded enthusiastically. "Thanks, mister!"

Later, once they'd finished their drinks and had some rough jerky from behind the counter to at least put something in their stomachs and the afternoon light outside was dimming to night, the trio lumbered upstairs, and inside the first door to the landing's right, where they found two smallish beds and a single window.

Jasper and Michelle wasted no time in taking off their boots and laying down to snooze, but Unity was long behind them – sat on the edge of the bed she'd agreed to share with the snake girl, and running over their journey so far over and over again in her head.

It was then, however, as the sunlight faded altogether and the glow of the moon began to piece through the room's window, that she noticed something sticking out of the dresser on her side of the bed. Paper. Letter paper, folded across the middle.

Reaching over with a frown, she pulled out the drawer, and found at least four other pieces of similar paper inside – all stamped, but with sealing wax unapplied.

Curious, Unity plucked up the one that had been hanging out, and began to read it from the top. There was no signature or address, but the words were in a fine, almost regal script, and flowed with grace across the page.

I know you will never answer these letters, for if you could I would not have the pain to write them, but I continue to pen them all the same. I have penned them for ten years, now. Archer – I have missed you every minute since you were stolen from me. I have tried to be strong... but I cannot live like you. I cannot hold honor and kindness. Not any longer. The pain is too great. I am sorry. This will be my last letter. For I must kill who I was – and become someone else. For you. To make this right.

Goodbye.

Shoving the letter back into the drawer with its companions and shutting it, Unity bit her lip hard, furrowed up her face, and laid back in bed with a thud hard enough to cause Jasper to stir and huff in confusion on the other side of the room. This woman... had been in pain. She had lost someone, just like she had lost Ms. Harper now. *Just like I never even had my mother – whatever happened to her.*

But one day I'll be strong enough. I'll understand these powers that Michelle says I have. Then I'll be able to save whoever I want.

8

Kijury stood at the door to his daughters' rooms – eyes closed, and head pressed against the frame. *Support her. Don't be overbearing.*

Despite his natural fatherly reservations, he supposed that this was a good thing. The girls trained so hard, after all, and while Amethyst seemed more than content to keep her head in study and the affairs of the castle, Justice had always been the more adventurous, ambitious, and - by extension - reckless one. She needed this, of that much he was certain.

Letting one last deep breath sift through his teeth, the deer opened his eyes and finally twisted his grip upon the handle.

A step later, and he was allowed a cautious glance at the room's interior – wooden walls, elegant furniture, and, sat before a dresser with an oval mirror atop it, was Justice – steadily combing at her long, flame-colored hair, and dressed in a flowing, dark green dress.

Kijury's face reflexively creased, and he moved up behind his daughter to reach for the comb. "Here, let me help you, sweetie."

But Justice merely tossed her head with a sigh. "I'm not a kid anymore, dad. I can do these things myself."

The deer shut his eyes for a second and nodded, retreating a little. "I know, I know. But I didn't think you'd go on a proper date so soon!"

Finishing off her brushing, Justice smiled back at her father. "Don't worry so much. Blurr is cute, and you liked him when you met him. Plus, we're just going to get something to eat. Speaking of which..."

She stood, took one last look in the mirror, and straightened her dress about her shoulders before turning and starting to make towards the chamber's door. "I should probably be down in the hall already to greet him."

At first Justice's father simply watched her move, but as she brushed past him, he laid his hand gently upon her shoulder - causing her to hesitate mid-step and turn about in confusion.

"Hey." Kijury inclined his head, pursing his lips as his brain tried to wrap itself around the conflict of powerful emotions he was feeling. "I'm proud of you, Justice. And I'm so glad to see you managing on your own. But we're here for you, okay? The Knights are too. If you need anything-"

"I know, Dad. Don't worry." Justice cut her father short, but smiled gently just afterwards. "But thank you."

Together, they made through the halls of the castle until they reached the entrance hall. A cheerful, booming voice made its way to their ears before they even stepped inside, and when they did do so, the room's most commanding presence soon made itself clear to their eyes.

Although Blurr was a year younger than Justice, the lion's golden-furred frame was tall, broad, and strong – accentuated well by the fine blue padded shirt that he wore. Destiny stood in the hall too – as slender and refined as ever, and accompanied, curiously enough, by a stoic Umi with a straight back and folded arms.

The opossum had been spending increasing amounts of time pacing nervously and sitting about the castle in what appeared to be deep introspection since the incident that had destroyed the orphanage.

As the ruckus they had heard earlier had led them to believe, the Queen and the lion appeared to be engaged in a friendly conversation, but the moment that Justice and her father came into sight, the feline glanced up, and a wide, warm grin spread across his face.

"There she is!" Blurr first spread his arms, then curtsied, then extended one hand in the approaching noblewoman's direction. "Justice. You look stunning.

And, of course-" He bowed his head to Kijury as Justice took his hand with a pleased giggle. "Your majesty."

The deer couldn't help but blush a little as he waved his hand to dismiss the title "That's not at all necessary. You know I said you could call me Kijury."

As the next few minutes of easy conversation unfolded, and Kijury watched closely, the warmth and connection between Justice and her date was clear. And, after he and Destiny exchanged silent, pleased glances of their own, he could feel his unease settling a little.

This is good for her. This feels... right.

Once the Queen's daughter and her date had left, with Kijury tagging along for a little longer to accompany them out of the castle grounds – as an excuse to conceal his reluctance to say goodbye for the evening, of course – Umi and the Queen found themselves alone in one of the castle's sitting chambers, except for the occasional knight or guardsmen.

At first the two simply resumed the attempt at easy company-keeping and light conversation that they had been maintaining earlier while waiting for Blurr's arrival, sat on two of the chamber's most comfortable crimson chairs, but the Queen eventually reached over and placed a gentle hand on the opossum's shoulder in concern. "Have you had any success as of yet?"

The opossum shook her head darkly, adjusting the arms of her leathers. "No. Not yet."

A long moment of silence, while Destiny allowed Umi to think, before the middle-aged knight sighed and rubbed at the bridge of her muzzle. "But she has to be out there somewhere. No body, no sign of her... and I can feel it."

She looked to Destiny, and met the Queen's eyes with dark meaning. "Not just her, either. I can sense a plot as well. Something awful, just out of reach. I know I need to act now – before things get worse – but at the same time I know that..."

Her gaze fell again. "Even if we found her - she doesn't even know I exist. What safety and reassurance could I possibly offer her?"

The Queen's grip on Umi's shoulder tightened. "It's never too late. Never."

"In fact, the two of you have more in common than you might know."

"What do you mean?"

"Well, you see – fifteen years ago, when you first arrived here-"

The explosion that followed those words was all too regular within Unity's nightly rumination. The fragments of stone, wood, and the upheaval of the earth all around her. It was a scene she'd been reliving over and over again ever since the day of the orphanage's destruction – and thus brought little more than a sigh to the cat girl's lips as she turned over in bed, determined to get some rest after all.

What was surprising, however, was when another explosion came. And another. Not within her dreams, but quite clearly from just beyond the room they were sleeping in, if the bed's slight shaking was to be believed.

Unity shot up straight in bed, and her first glance around her revealed that Jasper and Michelle had already done so themselves – craning their necks towards the space's single window, where a faint orange glow was still visible from beyond the slitted shutters.

Michelle caught Unity's eyes and shook her head. "Another of Glimmer's servants is here. A man. He's nearly found us."

Moving in unison without exchanging a further word, the trio leaped to their feet and began to ready themselves without exchanging words - Jasper drawing his sword, and Unity grasping Maple's axe from the side of the bed. A few seconds later they were clattering down the thin stairway to the common room, and out into the space itself, which was empty of even the bartender.

The midnight world that waited for them beyond the tavern's doors, however was far from empty. Confused and panicked denizens dashed to and fro up the settlement's street, yelling or screaming at one another, and the dancing, flickering light of a few small fires around the nearby buildings lit the scene with long, foreboding shadows.

"Get back inside, children. There's a dangerous man on the loose."

The voice came from the right, and the trio of young adventurers turned to see a tall, slim man in leather stood silhouetted by a blaze - the one that the bartender had called Manto last evening. His right hand was outstretched, and in it was a long blade of blue fire that contrasted powerfully with the red behind it.

And one thing's certain - if Manto is in town, trouble's not far behind.

Raising her voice so that it would carry over the ruckus all around, Unity crossed her arms – making sure to show off Maple's axe. "We know – that's what we're doing out here. He's after us, and he's not going to stop until he finds us."

But Manto wasn't hearing it – moving closer and raising his flame-blade bearing arm to gesture to the tavern. Now, Unity could see his eyes glisten a piercing blue much like the light of his weapon. "I said get inside! I am a knight of Penlight, and it is my responsibility to protect you!"

Before Unity could bite back further, however, there was a high-pitched whistle, and the cat girl, her companions, and Manto all staggered back as a projectile zipped through the space between them.

All else fell quiet in the street, and knight and young adventurers shifted as one – Michelle preparing her magic, and Jasper and Manto hefting their weapons – to see a single figure standing framed by the end of the street from which the trio had arrived the day prior. A hat sat upon his head, framing long canine ears, a sharp, thin muzzle poked out from beneath it, and to either side, his arms stretched out to point two smoking revolvers in their direction.

One step, two steps, three steps. The red-eyed coyote smiled wickedly with each pace he came closer to his targets, and kept his weapons unflinchingly trained in their direction.

"They call me the Hustler. Knew I'd be making your acquaintance soon enough." The rugged canid jerked his head and left revolver in Manto's direction, causing the knight to reflexively raise his blade. "And you're Manto, of course. Trust the Queen to send her cheapest bounty hunter of a Knight my way."

The knight growled, and his magic weapon blazed brighter. "If you think you're not destined for the castle's cells, you're dead wrong. Or just plain dead. Test me."

The Hustler raised both eyebrows beneath the brim of his hat, before squinting down the length of his guns. "Oh, gladly."

Manto was swift and smooth in raising his blade to deflect the coyote's oncoming bullets, but what he couldn't have seen coming was that the Hustler wasn't aiming for him at all – but rather a barrel just to the side of where the knight stood, leaned up against the building to the right of the tavern.

At first the knight simply frowned and seemed confused, but then a spark of light shone from within the barrel, and his eyes flew wide – only milliseconds before the barrel exploded, and Manto was sent flying back into a building on the other side of the street with a great crash of wood and stone.

Cackling loudly, the Hustler began to rain bullet after bullet upon Michelle and Jasper, with the snake girl parrying each one with her magic as she turned back to yell in Unity's direction. "Help Manto – we'll keep him busy!"

Nodding, the cat girl dashed over in the direction of where Manto had landed – soon finding the knight pinned beneath a large section of wooden wall. When she fell to her knees, gripped the edge of the object, and put her entire body into lifting, however, she found that it was far heavier than she expected, and fell back defeated with a cry of pain and exertion.

Manto, groaning in discomfort of his own, did his best to struggle in the meantime, but Unity was quickly losing hope, and began to shake her head. "I can't... lift this..."

But then the voice inside her head spoke back up for the first time in a while. *Oh, but yes you can. Just look inside. Listen to Michelle. You can do anything. Take anything. Everything you want.*

She gritted her teeth, closed her eyes, and placed her hands back on the edge of the wall. *I can. I can do this.*

The feeling that followed was one of the strangest she had ever experienced. Tingling, sparkling energy – rushing in from every inch of her body, from the tips of her fingers to the core of her chest – that made her feel like she was glowing. And, most of all, *powerful.*

This is magic. Michelle was right.

Before she knew it, slowly – ever so gradually – the wall was lifting up and off of Manto, and soon she cried out loud again and tossed it to the side completely – leaving the knight to scramble to his feet and look over at the cat girl with confusion in his eyes.

They had no time to exchange words, however, before the Hustler noted that Manto had recovered, and began sending one gun's worth of bullets over in their direction – causing Manto to summon his blade, and move back into combat while providing Unity cover.

As she glanced back over at her companions, she noticed Jasper looking over at her with his jaw hanging wide – in clear awe, while Michelle continued to deflect the rest of the Hustler's bullets.

"Unity – you have... powers? Like Michelle?" Face lighting up in enthusiasm, the wolf jerked his thumb towards Manto – who was steadily advancing on the coyote gunman assailing them. "Come. Try something like Manto. You can do it."

Nodding, Unity took advantage of a sudden lull in the gunfire as the Hustler backed up some and reloaded to close her eyes once more, and extend her hand. In her mind's eye, she could see it – a long, slender blade just like the knight's, formed out of the power that the voices in her head had promised her. She focused everything into it – her anger, her adrenaline, and her need to rise above...

And then, she felt it. That buzz of power again.

Her eyes jolted open, and she beheld the blade of her imagination in reality – pale-black, arched at the tip.

The cat girl could only smirk, and glance up to where the Hustler, Manto, and her companions were still playing a game of bullet-riddled back-and-forth.

Time to end this.

Although the Hustler was still grinning and seemed coolly confident at keeping his current assailants at bay with his constant stream of fire, he was clearly too occupied to be paying Unity mind, and thus the cat girl was able to slip off to the side at a low, crouched pace – keeping her glowing blade low so as not to give herself away through its light. Like this, she was able to come closer and closer to the coyote's side and back – using the cadence between his shots to step forward.

Things were going perfectly, until Jasper's gaze lingered on Unity's movement for a second long enough for the Hustler to take note, and the coyote wheeled about with one gun already outstretched and ready to push her back with gunfire.

Now or never.

Yet the cat girl moved quicker. Swooping in to move with the Hustler's side-step, Unity stayed behind him, looped her arm around, and caught the bandit's neck with her arm – pulling him backwards until she had him held fast, and her magic, illuminated blade at his throat.

The shots fell silent, and Unity's growl rose to replace them. "Drop the guns. Now."

For a long moment the Hustler said nothing, while Manto, Jasper, and Michelle waited paces away with their fighting stances ready to counter more attacks, before – huffing in a mixture of fear and anger – his hands loosened, and the twin weapons fell to the sand with matching thuds.

What followed happened even faster than the fight itself had. Manto dismissed his sword and swooped in to kick the Hustler's legs out from under him, and placed his foot on the coyote's back before he could try to push himself back up.

Stepping back, Unity watched with her heart bounding as the knight produced robes from his gear and began to bind the coyote's hands, and her own blade spluttered out as well – leaving her suddenly feeling deeply exhausted as all the energy that had charged within her left all at once. *So this is how Michelle feels after using her magic. Now I understand.*

"Should have known this was a bad job. Glimmer's gone too far, this time." Spitting into the sand as Manto finished fastening the binds and hauled him to his knees, the Hustler glared up at all those around him. "But my cards are out, it seems. Going to put me out of my misery?"

Manto scoffed and gave the bandit another rough tug. "I'm a bounty hunter, not a killer. Get on your feet."

The Hustler reluctantly complied, while Unity made over to rejoin her companions with a scoff of her own. "Not going to thank us?"

The knight shook his head and sighed, still preoccupied with keeping the Hustler's binds in check. "No need to be so sharp and hasty, young lady. But I do thank you for your help. Even though I could have handled this on my own."

Unity rolled her eyes. *Not likely. We all saw that.*

But then Manto finally met each of the three young adventurers' eyes in turn, and nodded sharply to acknowledge them. "Stay safe out here. World's a dangerous place with no-goods like this one around."

Then he turned on his heel, and began to pull the Hustler along behind him in the direction of the town's exit.

Jasper gave a quiet whoop of victory, and turned to 'high-five' Michelle, who returned the gesture despite looking just as exhausted as Unity felt. As they stood there watching Manto haul Glimmer's coyote servant away, however, the predominant thing Unity felt was pride swelling up within her chest. She had done it. She'd made the difference for once, and she had powers, just like Michelle had said.

Ah, but this is just the start, Unity. Just wait and see what you'll achieve...

9

— • —

Even by the time that the morning came around and the desert sun began to shine through the tavern room's window, Unity's mood had hardly improved. The combat in the middle of the night had left a dark taste, and the letters she'd read beforehand were still weighing on her mind.

Jasper rose from the bed and went about stretching to start the day with a smile and easy conversation on his lips, as chirpy as ever, but the cat girl remained sat at the edge of the bed for quite some time, deeply sobered by the thought of leaving the place where that unknown woman had last been.

What's the point of even trying, if it's so easy to ruin everything?

Eventually, however, she righted herself and made her way downstairs, where she found the main hall mostly empty, but for Michelle and Jasper at the bar enjoying some fresh fruit that – according to Jasper – had been free as a reward for their help in defeating the Hustler the night before.

Unity sat down and plucked up an apple that was surprisingly fresh for being out in the middle of the desert, but before she'd even taken her first bite, Michelle reached over across the bar and touched the cat girl's shoulder with a confused glance. "Something wrong, Umi? Is it your powers?"

Still feeling somewhat uncomfortable with the fact that her so-called powers were now common knowledge, Unity first scowled, but then shook her head. "No, I'm feeling just fine again. It's just that... last night... I found some letters. Got me thinking, is all."

The snake girl nodded, and didn't press further, but Unity's mood was already more ruined by being prodded.

*Thinking that we've already lost everything. And that if we don't do this right...
that we'll have nothing at all to show for it.*

After they finished eating and made out into the sweltering daylight sun, the
damage left by the Hustler's explosives was even more visible in the pale desert
daylight, and the burning that had continued after the initial attack had left its
own mark as well, but the occupants of the settlement were already about making
repairs, and paid the trio of young adventurers little attention as they made their
way down the street and out of civilization into the desert once more.

"Michelle? Are we still on Glimmer's tail? The snake nodded, and thus Unity
next turned to Jasper. "And what lies ahead?"

The wolf thought for a moment as he had before when they'd first entered
the desert – perhaps a little longer given the fact he was already visibly sweating
and about to start panting - before smiling and nodding. "The Attleway Bay, if I
remember correctly!"

Unity nodded, despite her inner incredulity. *How can he possibly remember so
much of the map? He really isn't right in the head.*

After so much time spent in the lifeless desert, arriving at the Attleway Bay's long,
rocky beach was a deep relief – even if it was a rather unappealing one, and the
only redeeming sight was the water of the bay itself, as well as the pale-blue mirage
of its other side atop it.

The change in scenery had done little to pep up Unity's mood, however, and
sand was still sand – meaning that their progress and treads were still labored and
frustratingly slow.

Michelle wasn't exactly helping things, either – bearing a perpetually bothered
expression, and eventually stopping altogether upon the dunes. "Glimmer's energy is fading. She's moving fast, across the other side of the coast. And we need
to as well, if we want to catch up with her."

Unity sighed out loud, and tossed up her hands at the sparkling water that stretched out just in front of them. "And how are we supposed to get over there? She has the map, and we don't. Of course she's moving faster." She turned around to look back at the wolf boy standing behind them with both eyebrows raised. "Jasper?"

Looking thoroughly sheepish, the young canine shrugged his shoulders. "I'm sorry – I only remember that the bay is here, and our path forward is, well… on the other side. But we'll get her, okay?"

The cat girl could only shake her head. *Just when we need his nerdiness most.*

They started off moving again, searching at the top of each dune to get as good of a look as they could across the coast in hopes of spotting some kind of building or natural bridge to allow them to cross the bay. They found none, however, and thus remained silent in growing demoralization until Jasper spoke up again. "She knows we're following, and she has to be worried, else she wouldn't have sent Maple and the Hustler to try to stop us."

Unity opened her mouth to dismiss the wolf's sugarcoating, but at that very moment, she spotted an unusually dense, high, and circular gathering of rocks at the bottom of the next dune, and frowned. "Are those..?"

Michelle, craning her longer neck even higher, nodded. "Caves."

The trio paced cautiously over to the opening in the rocks, and were soon able to see that the gap extended down further and further into the sand and gray until it dipped to the left, and ranged beneath the very water of the bay.

But the more they examined that dip, however, the more splits between the rocks appeared, until it became clear that this hidden grotto was almost honeycomb-like in complexity.

Unity sighed, and slapped her arms against her trousers as they came to a halt just before the slope. "There's so many ways we could go, and so much water. Either we'll get stuck, or waste even more time than going around the long way. This is hopeless."

Jasper and Michelle's silence in response to her defeatist statement did little to sweeten the cat girl's mood, and she soon raised her leg in preparation to stomp it down into the sand in frustration.

Before she could, however, there was a distinct rustling noise from amongst the rock formations in front of them, and Unity turned around to her companions with her ears perked up. "Was that you?"

Jasper blinked emptily, and Michelle shook her head. "No."

The cat girl turned her gaze back to the beach and rocks in front of her, and squinted amongst the rocks. *Sand... stone... shells... and... pink?*

Her eyes widened as she recognized eyes amongst the blob of salmon color peeking up above the outcropping in front of them – just in time for her jaw to drop as the eyes rose up further, and were soon accompanied by a neck, arms, and body.

It was a short, skinny girl that Unity could only assume was an axolotl – dressed only in bluish scraps of cloth that looked as though they had survived a shipwreck and more. *Probably have.*

Jasper and Michelle gasped but remained silent as the girl slowly, tentatively approached – seeming curious rather than frightened by their presence. Eventually, once she'd drawn near, she looked the trio up and down, and waved with a wide, toothless smile. "Hi there! My name is Bubbles. This is my home! What are you doing on the beach?"

Although the overwhelming emotion on her mind was relief that this new arrival wasn't one of Glimmer's servants or a new threat of some other kind, Unity couldn't help but groan internally at the chipper tone in the axolotl's voice. *She seems even worse than Jasper. I didn't think that was possible.* "We're travelling. And in quite a hurry too."

But then an idea occurred to the cat girl, and her perturbed expression turned to an ever so slightly wicked smile. "Say, Bubbles. If you live here, do you know a path to the other side of the bay?"

Bubbles' face lit up at the question, and Unity could already tell they'd found luck before the Axolotl had even spoken a word.

Gold tendrils cut through the water like glittering, curling skis – carrying Glimmer's robed form forward across the bay with supernatural speed.

Though she was forced to squint her eyes behind her hood as the fabric whipped about her head and neck, she could still see the silvery waves stretching out in front of her, as well as the land on the bay's opposite side just out of sight. *Close, but still too far. I have to move faster to be there waiting for them. Faster, or...*

At that very moment, something dark moving below the water just in front of her caught Glimmer's eye, and she glanced down amongst the flicking magic of her skis to see a long, angular silhouette gliding somewhere deep beneath her.

She smirked. "We can use a little something to make this more fun."

Allowing her magic to control her path forward and keep her aloft by itself for now, Glimmer closed her eyes and reached out with her mind – searching for the consciousness of the beast coasting along with her. When she found it, it resounded back to her – ancient and powerful, but also dull and instinctual. It had mistaken her for a bird of some kind gliding just above the waves, and was waiting for a moment to strike.

Molding its old, stubborn mind wasn't exactly easy, but before long she had drained out all base need and replaced it with two things – anger, and images of a certain girl's face.

Releasing the grasp of her magic and reopening her eyes, Glimmer focused back on the path before her and continued to glide forward with a wicked smile spreading beneath her robes as the dark shadow beneath peeled off to go back in the direction from which it had come.

"After all – if she is so easily slain, she wouldn't be of much use to me when the time comes."

10

After further introductions were exchanged – with Jasper's being most enthusiastic, of course - Bubbles took the lead as they ventured into the narrow cave walks and grottos that the axolotl assured them would lead to the other side of the bay, leaving Unity, Michelle, and Jasper to trail behind at an uneasy distance.

Although – despite the gap between them, Jasper failed to let up with his questions and curiosity for some time. "So, Bubbles... Where do you come from?"

Glancing over her shoulder with the same apparently endless energy that she'd been displaying ever since they'd met her, the scrappy-clothed axolotl shrugged. "I'm not quite sure! I've lived here since I was young. It was hard to fend for myself at first, but I got used to it."

Much like us, then.

The girl seemed innocent and honest enough, but Unity couldn't help but stay a little uneasy. They'd only encountered enemies along their journey so far, with the mostly nonplussed denizens of the village in the Arid Frontier aside, and they were also in deeply unfamiliar, dangerous territory here.

The deeper into the caverns they ventured, the darker the water that flowed around them grew, and the more and more the cat girl had to squint to make out her companions picking their way past larger stones before and around her.

Even Bubbles eventually slowed some when they came to a particularly tight neck in the cave walls, tilting her head back at Unity with a neutral, conversational expression. "I've never been further than this at this time of year. It's too dark to see."

The cat girl scoffed. "Yeah, I noticed."

But then her thoughts took a sudden, innovative turn, and she waved her hand in the air. "Wait a moment."

The others, Bubbles included, froze in the dim light and waited as requested as the cat girl closed her eyes, breathed deeply, and concentrated on her inner emotions and strength, just as she had last night upon saving Manto.

At first, nothing came whatsoever, and she could feel Jasper first bristle and then pipe up from next to her. "Unity?"

She tossed her head and ignored him – only concentrating harder, and extending her arm out into the darkness before them. *Come on. You can do this.*

"What are you doing, Uni?" Michelle – her voice uncertain and doubtful.

"Giving us some light."

Fueled by her determination to prevail and prove her capability, the cat girl's body sang with energy, and before she knew it, the blade of magic she'd summoned yesterday began to extend from her palm – shining white despite its dark hue, and bathing just enough light upon the cavern walls to allow them to see forward where they needed to go.

Jasper, Bubbles, and even Michelle seemed impressed and glad to have solved their problem, but as soon as they started moving again – using the blade's magic flame to light the way – Unity noticed the snake girl watching Bubbles closely from behind, almost as though she were sizing her up.

Moving as close as she could without bumping into her with her summoned weapon, Unity whispered into her companion's ear. "What's wrong? What are you doing?"

Michelle's answer was as deadpan and – much to Unity's frustration – full volume as usual. "Examining our new companion."

The cat girl scoffed. "And yet you seemed to trust Jasper immediately."

The snake girl shrugged. "We didn't exactly have a choice at the time. And besides..." she gave an offhand gesture in the wolf boy's direction as he trotted along with a happy-go-lucky stride.

Unity had to stifle a mean-spirited giggle at that. *Yeah. Hard to assume malice from someone who acts like a newborn pup.*

Although she supposed he wasn't all that bad. Almost endearing, really, if one looked past the optimism and the endless fact-spouting to the warmth of his smile, his stalwart nature, and the shine of his light gray fur...

That caught Unity up short and caused her to scowl at the stupidity of her wandering thoughts. *This is Jasper we're talking about – the stupid, blabbering wolf boy.*

Thankfully she didn't have to ridicule her mind for much longer, however, before a distraction demanded her attention. The way ahead of them was opening up into a space much, much higher than the meager light of her blade could illuminate, and the rock floor beneath them had split into two paths that seemed to outline a large, deep pool in the cave's center.

It was at the edge of that pool that the scaly, flat body sat. It was some kind of larger fish with a slim, angular form, and seemed to have died freshly, too, as fresh blood was still running from the pierced wounds along its side.

Unity scoffed – walking over and lashing out to kick the carcass's side with her boot. "Huh. Something had a bad day."

As she glanced back over her shoulder at the others, however, she found Michelle and Jasper to have concerned expressions on their faces, and Bubbles's face to be dead straight in contrast to the enthusiastic, mostly happy-go-lucky demeanor the axolotl girl had held so far – almost as though she'd seen a ghost.

The cat girl frowned in their newfound companions' direction. "What's wrong?"

The axolotl said only one word. "Bait."

Unity's frown deepened. "What do you mean? Do you want us to fish with this?"

Bubbles shook her head. "No. That. Bait. And now you..."

A great, deep roar came from the waters below them – rumbling in the cave walls so deeply that they could feel it through their feet, and causing all four youths to freeze where they stood – watching what little they could of the pool in the chamber's center with wide eyes.

"Something's coming." Michelle began to pool magic in the palms of her hands, as she had so many times in preparation for battle over these short few days. "It's not Glimmer's... but she'd controlling it. I can sense her magic."

But then the roar came again – much closer now – and Unity only had time to take a step back from the pool before a shadow made itself apparent from beneath the still surface, and then the room erupted into chaos.

At first the cat girl thought she'd seen only one form burst from the pool, but then one, two, three snarling, snapping heads lashed out in their direction one after the other, and she thought that maybe a small swarm had come forth.

But that assumption too was soon to be proved wrong, as the beast finally came to settle atop the water and face the adventurers in its entirety. Its body was thick and long, and at its shoulders, no less than four individual necks sprouted forth – each carrying a head with two glowing, golden eyes.

Unity raised her blade higher – casting light upon the thing's form just as the heads all reeled back to strike at once. *A water hydra. I remember from my books.*

In the next few seconds, everything happened. Bubbles screaming and leaping back up into the caverns from where they had come. Jasper roaring, drawing his sword, and parrying one head's advance with enough strength to successfully send it into the grotto's wall. Michelle weaving her hands in the air, and twisting the middle two so that they never reached her at all.

Unity's own head seemed even more unruly than its compatriots, however, and struck in quick, sharp succession – forcing the cat girl to stay on her toes and parrying twice as fast as her companions. Eventually she was able to land a few solid strikes with her magic blade, but soon she realized, much to her frustration, that they hadn't even marked the beast's scales.

Soon after, Jasper's strained voice carried to her across the cacophony of thudding, snarls, and cries echoing throughout the grotto. "We can't kill this thing, we can't! Everything we're throwing at it is just bouncing off!"

Michelle's voice came soon after. "I think I can do something about that!"

Although Unity didn't have the time to glance over to watch her in action, a few seconds later Michelle's black, sand-like magic spouted forth and began to wrap itself around the Hydra's heads like small orbs. And, just like that, the golden glow within the beast's eyes dimmed – almost like Michelle's magic was dulling out Glimmer's.

"Her command is gone! Go!"

Wasting not a second to heed Michelle's command, Unity sprang forward. Taking advantage of the beast's momentary disorientation, she wove in between its heads and necks, dodged one wayward swipe from its left flipper at the pool's edge, and let out a sharp cry as she first pulled back her magic blade and then plunged it into the Hydra's chest – causing it to let out a groan of its own and reel back in agony.

Deed done and blow dealt, it was all Unity could do to scramble back and try to keep out of the way of the hydra's heads' last flails as its body went limp, and its necks were dragged back towards the pool's edge.

Before long she was standing clear by Michelle and Jasper's side as the former dispelled her magic and the latter sheathed his sword - watching the beast sinking below the pool's surface.

You'll have to do better than that, Glimmer. The second I get my hands on you, you're finished.

11

— . —

Hydra defeated, shaky breaths caught, and frightened Bubbles retrieved from the tunnels behind them, the four youths organized themselves around the light of Unity's blade as best as they could, and tried to wring-dry the parts of their clothing that had gotten soaked during the fight.

They'd gotten as much sea water out as they thought possible after a few minutes, and resumed their march as quickly as they could – a little worse for wear after the sudden exhaustion, but not at all eager to remain in the dark, wide cave with the hydra's corpse.

Although she'd seemed perturbed before and during the fight itself, Bubbles' cheerful demeanor didn't take long to return, and soon she was practically skipping ahead as their path through the caves and rocky walls began to slowly slope upwards again – occasionally glancing back at her companions as she went. "If we're lucky, we'll find something for lunch!"

Jasper smiled at that, and turned to Unity and Michelle in clear hope of eliciting a similar reaction. "That sounds nice!"

A few seconds later, however, the axolotl's eager eyes dipped down to another, much smaller pool in the cave's floor, and she suddenly dropped down into a crouch to first stick out her arm and then pull it back roughly – producing a small, still thrashing fish and holding it out towards Unity with a triumphant air. "Here!"

It was all the cat girl could do to keep herself from emptying her stomach on the spot in response to the wriggling creature's sight and smell. "No, uhm, thanks. We're not all that hungry."

A few minutes later, and the unthinkable happened – a dot of light appeared ahead of them further down the tunnel, and soon blossomed brighter and brighter until Unity was able to dismiss her blade of light altogether, and they eventually ambled out into the open air once more – relieved both to see real sunlight again, to finally be out of the caverns, and to have reached their destination.

This beach wasn't as wide or thick as the one from which they had come, which Unity was thankful for, as she felt that she'd go crazy if they had to labor their way through any more sand. Just as the ground was starting to firm up and turn to root-bound soil, however, the cat girl looked back to see that Bubbles had hesitated some steps behind them, and was tilting her head at the ground with clear confusion and conflict.

Soon, Jasper and Michelle turned too, and the axolotl looked up at them in question. "I've never... gone this far. I'm not even sure if I can."

Jasper beamed and beckoned forward. "Come on, sure you can! Just try!"

A moment's further hesitation later, and the axolotl did as told – but immediately sprung back with a giggle under her breath when her foot touched grass. "It feels funny!"

Unity looked over to Jasper and lowered her voice. "Do we really think she can come along?"

She and the wolf boy locked gazes for a long moment, before Jasper sighed with uncharacteristic sobriety and shook his head. "We can't take her. It's too dangerous for her. At least, yet."

"Jasper is right." Michelle chimed in, nodding her serpentine head. "But we'll come back for her."

Unity couldn't help but scoff with a little irony at hearing that.

"On our way back, right? Once we win."

Walking amongst the vines and stumps of the jungle floor would have taken far, far too long, especially with the rain beginning to patter down around her… but thankfully, she needed to do no such thing. Thanks to her magic, Glimmer was able to spring from treetop to treetop – cushioning each arching step with a shining platform of gold.

She was gaining ground fast – just as she'd hoped she would. The boy's map was illuminating, yes, but she'd still have to find the entrance to the caverns, and then work her way down into them before the children arrived. Sending another obstruction their way might be entertaining… but the rain was quickly becoming a nuisance even for her, and she didn't want to risk things right now. Not when her plan was working so well.

Better than she could have dreamed, in truth. It was easier – and safer – to take her along than to take her by force or magic. To go about this any other way would have been foolish. If she took control now, it would only be a matter of time before the girl broke free. *Too early. Too early for this plan to work.*

But no. She was certain. She had waited and thought for long enough. If she did this right. If she waited, was patient, and did this right…

Glimmer smirked darkly as the faintly flickering lights of a lantern-lit settlement appeared amongst the flood of rain beginning to batter harder and harder against her sodden robes and leaping, bounding form. *If the map tells true, as it has so far… then I'm as good as there.*

"Just one spring of the trap later, and I'll have it all. Upholder, her kingdom, and her whole line will fall."

It'll stop soon enough. That's what Michelle had said as she'd watched the first raindrops fall through the roof of the jungle they'd found themselves in since the sun had begun to set, with some splashing upon her scales to wet them shiny.

But, despite Michelle's reassurance, the rain hadn't stopped – and by the time that they had made through the jungle's vines and branches for half an hour, thunderclaps were ringing in their ears every few seconds, and rain had soaked through every layer of clothing that they had.

And yet, they still pushed on – the knowledge that they were close driving them past exhaustion, and past the fact that it was night, and they had hardly slept properly the night before thanks to the Hustler. Bubbles had been reluctant to see her newfound friends go, and it'd been hard for even Unity to leave behind someone that had proved to be so sweet within such a short period of time, but they knew they needed to keep moving at all costs.

Despite their determination, however, the worst part was that – at least, until Unity piped up – nobody was speaking to break up the monotony and the constant drum and weight of the rain. Not even Jasper.

"Aren't you going to hum a song or share dumb facts, pooch? Bit dull."

At first Jasper failed to respond, but then, after they'd pulled and struggled their way through a particularly challenging patch of vines, he looked back with an expression that seemed almost genuinely hurt. "Why do you always talk like that?"

Unity blinked, and raised her voice over a particularly loud thunderclap. "Like what?"

"Like... you know." The wolf shrugged.

They went back to walking in silence for a long few moments while Unity's brain worked over itself against the background of the rain, before she sighed and threw up her hands. "I'm sorry. I know I can be... a bit much sometimes. It's just that..."

The cat girl trailed off, not finding any way that she could finish the sentence without sounding pathetic and making her apology far more sincere than she was prepared to.

Jasper, however, didn't press further, and simply nodded – causing the water that had built up in his head fur as they had been moving to spray off. "It's okay. You've both been through a lot. And..." The wolf boy shrugged again. "It's the least I can do to be here and help. It's why I came, after all."

That brought Unity a little smile, although she neglected to reply out loud. *Maybe it really isn't so bad having some backup around. Even if it talks a lot more than Michelle.*

Before she could linger on the odd feeling of relief and release that this interaction had brought her, however, Unity soon found her feet grinding to a halt – followed closely by that of her two companions. *What is... that?*

At first Unity thought that the mass blocking their way was just the base of some ancient, particularly thick tree, but then there was a shift of movement, and she could see that it had arms and legs. Two, four, six...

A spider. A tarantula man.

The cat girl's heartbeat quickened as a thick-furred head with dark eyes that glinted in the dim jungle lighting and the occasional flashes in the sky leaned down from above, and looked her closely in the face.

Then the creature spoke with a voice as deep and dark as the thunder. "This is no place for you, children."

Although she backed up a few steps in a mixture of reflex and fright, Unity wasted no time in raising her hands and preparing herself to summon her blade – despite the fact that she was still drained from fighting the hydra and lighting up the grottos earlier in the day. "Another servant. Do you work for Glimmer too?"

"Glimmer?" The name was followed shortly by a bright flash of lightning that revealed more of the tarantula man's body – his muscular torso, his arms, and the jagged features of his half-human face.

He frowned and shook his head slowly. "Child, that name bears no meaning to me. Mine is Khentor Graves, and I am simply the protector of this jungle and all that move through it. As such, I cannot let you pass. The way ahead is treacherous, especially in this weather, and there are many who live there who are far more dangerous and far less amiable as I."

Unity gritted her teeth, and took a step closer to the much larger beast – puffing out her chest in an attempt at intimidation. "We've been through worse. Now step aside."

Yet the tarantula simply shook his head – as calm and measured as ever. "You are young, and I cannot allow this."

"Come, Unity. Maybe he's right - we'll find another way."

But Jasper's voice from behind did nothing to cool Unity's mood, nor bring reason to her mind. *Glimmer isn't waiting, so why should we?*

Instead, she threw out both of her arms, and reached deep into her chest with her mind to tear out the tingling energy there with as much determined fury as she could muster. "We. Want. To. Get. *Through!*"

The yell was enough to cause even the physically fearsome tarantula man to lean back some on his eight legs, and Unity used that opening to lash out with her collected power – sending out silvery, glowing binds that wrapped about and around Khentor's many legs to keep them in a tangle, and even his mouth shut - so that the tarantula could only thrash and grunt wordlessly where he had been standing.

Unity gave his noises no mind, however, and simply strode past him at furious speed – gesturing over her shoulder for her companions to follow. "Come on. Now. Glimmer is getting away."

Jasper and Michelle, although both uneasy and exchanging slightly unnerved glances, could only think to scramble after – leaving the tarantula man to struggle behind them.

The weather, however, was not so obedient. Not only did the rain only strengthen once they'd begun to continue along their way, but the occasional thunder that they'd heard before soon became a regular, ground-shaking roll.

At first Unity responded by pushing harder and faster with every boom and bolt, but even she began to flinch and glance up at the sky through the vines above them as the storm grew more and more intense, until there were barely seconds between strikes, and the very ground felt as though it was prickling with energy.

Eventually, after the latest crack felt as though it had hit ground mere feet away, Unity cursed under her breath and turned to her companions with a yell. "Glimmer is doing this! She must be close!"

Scales slick and cottons dripping, Michelle shook her head. "No. This isn't Glimmer. Something else is-"

Cutting the snake girl off, the latest bolt of electricity wove its way down out of the jungle's treetops – at first curving to the right, but then arcing back between branches, causing Unity's eyes to fly wide. *Is it..?*

A great, blinding flash, and then there was...

Nothing. No determination, no loss, no lust for revenge. Just darkness and forgetfulness.

12

—·—

*W*ake up, Unity. There's no time to sleep. Not now. Now is the time to let us in.

The savannah cat girl's eyes shot open, but when she did, they found nothing but darkness. Her limbs, too, could sense little – just comfort, stillness, and, above all, a consuming warmth that brought deep, deep relief from the foggy memories of cold and wet that hung at the edges of her mind. She could still smell damp and the lingering scent of rain, but for now...

Everything was calm.

The slightest twinge of confusion sparked within her. *Calm. That's strange. I remember being... angry.*

But then there was light – splitting open in front of her, and running down towards her stomach – and she squinted hard as pain split through her head. *Just five more minutes...*

"You're awake, my child! So early?"

Unity's frown deepened. "What..? Who..."

The voice came again. "Why! Your mother, of course!"

That made Unity frown, though her eyes remained closed, and her thoughts muddled. *That's wrong.* But why it was wrong, why this felt wrong... she couldn't quite remember. For all she knew, she had been up here in the treetops with her mother for as long as she'd been alive.

"Now, again – it's far too early for you to be awake. Sleep in just a *little* more, while mother fetches something to eat. For us all to eat, of course."

Sleep *did* seem awfully tempting... and Unity could almost feel herself giving in, and consciousness fading away altogether.

But then, just at the very brink of sleep, her lidded eyelids caught the outline of a dark shape moving over her, and – in low, foggy detail...

A fearsome, hungry, fanged face.

The cat girl's heart stopped beating, but she forced herself to remain stock still until the shape vanished, and she felt the ground beneath her shift a little as though the face's owner had moved away.

Once she was fairly certain she was in the clear, Unity's eyes shot open the rest of the way, and she pushed herself up from her lying position enough to finally get a look at her surroundings.

Her brain was still painfully slow, but the fear that continued to sink down into her very bones at what she now saw was enough to pull her to her senses faster and faster.

The creature whose face she had seen was indeed a little further away, and facing away from her... but from its crooked, arched, bony back, and the sparse-feathered wings stretching out above the arms there... she didn't have to see more to identify what it was.

A harpy. A predator of animal and human alike. The Kingdom had to drive them out from the villages when I was smaller.

In that moment, Unity knew that she had to act fast, and began to scan her surroundings further. Above her was only sky, and the rough, vine-woven 'basket' that lay beneath her and the beast appeared to be a nest of sorts. Jasper and Michelle were visible just a few feet away - laid upon the floor of the nest side by side – and both had their eyes open, but from their dazed and disoriented expression, it was clear that they were in the same daze she too had been until seconds ago.

One last deep, steadying breath later, Unity poised herself for movement, desperately tried to seek her powers, and shouted at the top of her lungs.

"Michelle! Jasper! She's going to eat us!"

The wolf and snake jolted up and began to glance about in urgent confusion, but the harpy was quicker – screeching out with enough volume to force Unity to clasp at her ears, and turning around to show her terrifying, gnarled face in full detail. Half avian, and half that of an old woman, the visage was drawn out, wrinkled, and its mouth was a mess of sharp, pointed teeth.

"I told you to go to *sleep*!"

The harpy raised her arm to carve across with a sharp, wicked strike, and at first Unity thought that she was done for. Just before the blow could land, however, the cat girl threw up both her arms, shut her eyes hard, and let out every last drop of energy she had within her out – through her mouth in the form of a scream, and from her palms in the form of booming, repulsing magic.

Caught off-guard mid-movement, the harpy was launched to the other side of the nest and lost its feet completely – landing on its back with a loud crash of vines and branches.

Recovering herself from a renewed wave of debilitating fatigue to use what little time she had as the harpy scrambled to recover its footing, Unity darted over to her companions, where Michelle was rising to a kneel, and Jasper was already on his feet – head darting to and fro as he assessed the situation.

Meeting the cat girl's eyes with some residual confusion, Michelle shook her head. "U-unity. I'm sorry - I don't have the magic right now. We need to do this the hard way."

Unity's face fell. "Neither do I. That was my last for the moment."

Before either of the girls could say or do more, however, Jasper unsheathed his sword – and just in time, too, as the harpy had righted herself and whipped about with far more speed than Unity had anticipated.

In turned out that her speed was to her detriment, however, as it gave Jasper the chance to whip his blade about and stick it into the harpy's side with a great roar – causing the beast to rear back with another ear-piercing screech.

Gritting her teeth and ignoring the pain the sound brought her, Unity turned about and began to search the edge of the nest for the strongest and thickest vine she could see.

Eventually she found one, and wasted not time in first hefting it up into both of her arms, and wheeling about to cast it through the air in the harpy's direction – hoping desperately that it would catch her, slow her down, or maybe even get her tangled like she'd been able to do to Khentor with her magic.

And, by some blessed miracle, it did – curling around with almost uncanny precision to first cause the creature to lurch back, and then let out a distressed cry as its wings were bound, and it began to stumble backwards in disorientation.

At first the trio of adventurers felt their hearts drop into the pits of their stomach as the harpy's struggling footsteps caused the nest to rock perilously, but then the creature's back leg missed the edge of the platform altogether, and then – with one last attempted flutter – it slipped over, and was gone.

The harpy's fall lasted almost too long, before they finally heard the great, trunk-shaking crash of her bound body hitting the floor, and the silence after that marked the end of her screeching.

Unity scowled, and shook her head darkly. "I have no mother."

For the longest moment after that sound, the trio simply stood there in the beast's nest – panting, glancing to one another, and still clearing their thoughts to shake the last of the lightning and the harpy's influence out of their minds.

Although Unity didn't say anything, and neither did Michelle, the few glances that the two girls shared made it clear that they both had the same thoughts. *That was... uncomfortable. Not to mention far too close.*

The first to come back to his senses fully, Jasper moved over the edge of the nest, and tentatively peeked down at the ground below. "Now to get down from up here, before more of her kind come along. Plus, we're... not far, I think. There's a village on the other side of the jungle, and then we've arrived at the Abyss Caverns. Where the Sun Skewer is supposed to be."

Moving back from the edge, he tilted his head at Unity in question. "Do you think you could help us, Unity?"

The cat girl nodded, and after a few minutes of brainstorming and collecting vines, she and the others had fashioned belts of a kind, which they slung out over the network of thin but sturdy trunks about and below the nest, and used to slowly rappel down, just like the cat girl had done a few times along the side of the orphanage.

All the while, Unity couldn't help but let her mind wander to the harpy's tricks and games – to mothers, Ms. Harper, and even the possibility that, just maybe, her real mother was out there somewhere. She had no way to know after all.

That thought, however, was out of line enough to cause her to shake her head and focus on their descent. No more time for distractions and stumbles. No more time for games, and distractions like this stupid Harpy.

They were going to find Glimmer, get their revenge, and put an end to whatever her evil plans were once and for all.

It seemed almost impossible – but eventually they touched solid ground once more, fought their way free of the jungle, and the blue of the sky became visible above the hills and treebanks ahead of them.

Before long, the foliage disappeared altogether – leaving them stood before a stunning vista of plains, visibly cultivated farmland, and, beyond it all, a tall, proud mountain range.

A few hours of navigating the scarce few rough, cartwheel-worn paths that wound through the landscape later, and they came to the edges of a farming settlement – utterly unlike that which they had found in the Arid Frontier in that it was at least the size of a town, had carts moving in and out of it at a somewhat regular pace, and appeared to be populated by more regular folk versus the nomads and vagrants earlier.

Just as they moved past the settlement's first ornate wooden houses, which each had friendly-looking gardens and trellises, Jasper pointed out a hand-carved wooden sign just to the side of the road. "Guardright. Then we're close! On the map, the Dancing Caverns and the Skewer right there, up against the mountains!" His hand moved to point instead to the peaks behind the silhouette of the town.

Unity said nothing as they continued to weave their way through Guardright, although her brain worked at full speed. *So it's really coming close. If we're right, and this is where Glimmer is headed... then there'll be nothing between us and her, before long.*

After a while, Michelle mirrored her thoughts alongside reaching out to pull Jasper back from being about to curiously wander off to inspect a flower by the side of the now partially cobbled avenue they were making down. "We might be safe for now, but keep your guard up. The Skewer might be close, but so is Glimmer. She could attack again at any moment."

The cat girl couldn't help but nod in agreement, though neither of her companions turned to see. *Who knows how many servants she still has left to send our way...*

Although it was definitely doing their stress and strain good to be amongst regular people again after their extended time in the wilderness, their fatigue definitely wasn't going away by itself, and thus they soon set themselves to finding somewhere that they could lodge for the night – eventually arriving at a flat building that seemed like more of an inn than the tavern where they had slept in the Arid Frontier.

After entering, taking in the small but cozy atmosphere of the fireplace-lit common room, and approaching the desk behind which the inn's human steward sat reading and smoking a pipe, Unity tried her best to put on a smile and use her crossed hands to hide the ruined state of her sundress. "Hi! We've travelled from Penlight, and would like a room for the night. But... we don't have any coin."

Looking up from his book, the steward gave each of the adventurers a long, good look up and down. "Penlight, ey? You three 'ave come far, haven't ya?" His eyes narrowed. "Don't tell me you're here for the caverns, like the rest of 'em."

Unity's jaw opened, but no words came out, and after a few seconds the steward simply sighed. "Thought as much. Well, little I can do except offer you a place. Could be your last night, after all."

The human placed his book down, and used the hand that had been holding it to gesticulate with conviction. "But first, let me tell you. We here have lived at the base of this mountain and the mouth of those caves for centuries. Ye think there remains something to be found down there?"

The trio of young adventurers had no answer, and the human tossed his head as a result before continuing his bitter rant. "There's nothing down there. Nothing. Yet kids like you are more interested in running off to die under the rock than living out their lives."

He leaned across his desk, took a deep puff from his pipe, and let it waft out into the three's faces. "But there's no dissuading ye', that much I know. I've said this piece what feels like a thousand times before. Just know one thing."

"The place brings nothing but death. No soul who's ever set foot inside has ever returned, and no matter how strong you think yourselves, ye'll be no exception. Mark my words."

Their sleep in the inn room's single, cramped bed was brief and fitful, and the morning came with a deep sense of destiny and dread that could be felt heavily between each of the three companions. They readied themselves and inspected their clothes and boots in silence – with Unity silently bemoaning the by now ragged state of her dress – and made their way downstairs to the inn's common room.

No breakfast reward awaited them, unlike that which they'd been treated to in the Arid Frontier, and the steward wasn't even behind his desk – leaving them with no other choice but to walk through the door and back out onto the hard road – literally, and metaphorically.

The village looked even more alive and comforting in its mundane nature in the morning light, which made the thought and act of stepping out beyond its borders to return to the grasslands almost impossibly hard.

Half of Unity wished that they could simply stay in Guardright, heed the innkeeper's words, and start a new life there, far away from all danger and struggle.

But the other half knew that there was no turning back now, and only burned hotter as they forged on and drew closer and closer to the foot of the mountains.

And then... they saw it. A round, arched break in the steep stones that made up the central peak's foot, and led in and down as far as their eyes could see – much like the entrance to the grotto which they had traversed with Bubbles.

The trio came to a gradual halt, and Michelle slowly nodded her scaly head. "This is it. The caverns."

One after the other, they exchanged glances. In Jasper's eyes Unity saw determination, bravery, but also a touch of fear and worry. Though whether for the wolf boy himself or for their quest, she couldn't tell. And in Michelle's...

She could only see a deep, inscrutable resignation that spelled out the innkeeper's words within her mind.

Ye'll be no exception. Mark my words.

13

— · —

It didn't take long for the darkness of the caves to begin to feel suffocating, and for the little light that Unity was able to cast with her abilities to feel insufficient. They could only see a few feet of featureless, stony walls out ahead of themselves, and the only thing that the cat girl herself could hear above the thudding of their steps and her heart was the voices in her head.

You're moving closer to doom with every step, Unity. But it's alright. We'll be here to catch you when you fall.

"What if the innkeeper was right?"

Unity knew she was being a devil's advocate by saying it, but she hadn't been able to keep it in any longer. The hopelessness of the dark, and the thought that Ophin knows how many others had already lost their way and even their lives down here was simply too much, despite all that they'd already been through.

Before Jasper could pipe back with the optimistic retort she expected from him, however, Michelle came to a dead stop just ahead of them – bearing an expression more revealing and plainly frightened than she had used throughout the entire time that Unity had known her.

"I can sense it. The Skewer."

Jasper gasped, face falling in turn. "And that means…"

Michelle nodded. "That Glimmer was right too. She knows where it is as well."

The trio stood in the magic-lit caverns in silence for a few moments, processing this revelation. That they were so close. That they had, after everything, truly arrived at their destination, which had once felt so intangible and distant.

Amongst the triangle of their fleeting, nervous eyes, one unspoken sentiment was unanimous. *So this is really happening.*

Unity, however, couldn't help but also feel a little frustrated that she couldn't sense the Skewer as well, so that she could lead the charge. *I want to find Glimmer first. I want my revenge to be the first thing she feels.*

The cat girl tried to pull herself together as Jasper broke the silence and insisted that they keep moving, but despite her deep breaths, and despite her attempts to simply focus on lighting the way ahead, she couldn't stop the voice in the back of her head creeping in with an almost smug inflection.

Oh, you'll have your chance...

Half an hour and a few forks in the way later, where they were forced to look to Michelle and allow the snake woman to carefully sense the correct path forward, the trio was deeper in the caverns than ever before, and feeling the building tension, anticipation, and claustrophobia of the situation more than ever as well.

As such, it was nothing short of transformative and a rush of fresh air as their next few steps found them walking slightly downhill, and the way ahead of them unexpectedly opened up in all directions – revealing a large, spherical space bathed in supernatural light, and intermittently broken up by long, perfectly round pillars running from ground to roof.

Part of the space's surface was rough, untamed rock just like the caverns from which they had just emerged, but a large, square section in the very center had been cleared and chiseled almost to perfection, and in the center of that space was a long, white staff with a jagged, hooked head, and a visible, glistening 'shield' of sorts around it, which seemed to be in part contributing to the uncanny light filling the cavern all around them.

Unity took one step ahead of her companions, jaw falling at the sight of the artifact just ahead of them. "That's..."

"The Sun Skewer, yes."

The trio turned as one to see an all-too-familiar robed figure striding into view from the side of the chamber with her hands folded in her lap in an almost gloating fashion.

"Glimmer." Jasper stepped forward in front of his two companions, and put his hand on the hilt of his sword.

The figure's head quirked to the side at that. "You paid attention. Good. Although, I expected no less from you, after how easily you tossed aside my obstacles." She stopped moving forward, and spread her folded arms. "Although that was undoubtedly all thanks to you, Michelle, wasn't it?"

Unity's face fell first with confusion, and then with shock. *How did she..?*

Michelle mirrored the cat girl's thoughts with her voice – dark magic beginning to pool in the palms of her hands. "How do you know my name?"

At first Glimmer only let out a low, sardonic chuckle, before reaching up to slowly, slowly pull her dark hood back...

To reveal the long, gray, scaled features of a rattlesnake with piercing golden eyes.

"A mother *always* knows her daughter. Especially when that daughter is oh-so-easy to find."

Michelle's reaction wasn't visible from Unity's perspective, but the cat girl's own was drastic enough on its own. Her jaw fell open, and her mind ground to a halt. *She didn't... mean me? This entire time? She meant Michelle? Michelle is... her daughter?*

When Michelle finally did speak up, it was in the most weak and broken voice that they had ever heard her use. "W-what do you mean? I..."

But Glimmer didn't wait long for her words to sink in – taking advantage of their stunned shock by reaching out in her daughter's direction with one hand, and spitting out a streaming jolt of golden magic which struck the snake girl in the center of the chest before fanning out and changing color – transforming into wispy, black sand.

Stepping forward in distress, Unity summoned her magic blade and called out in her companion's direction. "Michelle? What's happening?"

But Michelle didn't respond. Once the swirling settled some, leaving Michelle stood still in its center, Glimmer cackled and spread her arms in triumph. "Vulnerable, and malleable. Just as I'd hoped. You've all played along just wonderfully."

Unity's heart stuttered. *She's controlling her. Her magic...*

Turning away from them as though they were mere insects and beginning to pace away in the direction of the Skewer and the shield that surrounded it, Glimmer tossed her newly revealed serpentine head, and Michelle began to follow after her at a limp-legged, almost undead-like pace. "I felt so lucky when I sensed your powers at that backwater orphanage. You gave yourself up without even knowing."

Arriving within arm's length of the shield with Michelle not far behind, Glimmer reached out to almost touch it, and sighed. "But now our little game has come to an end. I could have done this alone, yes. You *were* expendable. But the strain would have taken far too long to recover from. Days, even. But now..."

She turned and beckoned to her 'daughter'. "I can do what needs doing immediately. Michelle?"

Unity and Jasper could only watch on in horror as their companion nodded, moved to the side, and raised both arms to begin channeling magic, just as she had done so many times to protect them. From the side, they could finally see her eyes – glowing golden.

"Yes, mother."

Before a few seconds had passed, Michelle's black, almost fluid-like magic had begun to spread out and wrap around the shield in the same way that it had wrapped around the hydra's heads. As a result, the supernatural light that had previously been filling the chamber dimmed, giving it a far more sinister energy, and causing Jasper and Unity's tension to raise yet further as they glanced between one another as though expecting the other to know what to do – half stuck with fear, and half stuck with indecision.

But then tangible, sparkling energy flooded the air – from without, rather than within like Unity's magic – and they both knew it was too late. The shield shattered with no warning – letting out a booming shockwave that caused a few of the space's outer pillars to first shudder and then start collapsing in on themselves with a great crashing and clattering.

Glimmer, however, seemed to completely ignore the chaos and calamity all around her, and simply stepped forward with her arms still outstretched as Unity and Jasper simply struggled to keep their balance on the shuddering ground.

"By Ophin have I earned this."

As soon as the words had left her serpentine lips, and her hands clasped around the Sun Skewer's shaft, a blinding pulse of energy shot out of the hovering artifact – blinding Unity and Jasper, and causing them to stagger back from the sheer force of wind rushing past them.

The sharp, golden light shone on and on as the two remaining companions tried their best to keep their footing and stay aware, but the scene that revealed itself to them when their vision finally returned did little to reassure them. Michelle stood stock still exactly where she had earlier, but Glimmer...

Was hovering in the center of the room now – the Skewer in her hand, a long, cruel smirk spreading across her serpentine face, and golden energy more powerful and volatile than ever emanating and crackling about her.

"Now, I have it. I have it all. I have *everything* I need. Penlight, its Queen, and all within and without it will bow before me."

Jasper and Unity could only huddle together at the sight and back further away towards the gap in the chamber wall through which they had come – brains whirling with everything that had just happened, and a tide of crushing defeat. *She has it. She has the Skewer. We failed.*

Before Glimmer could advance or say more, however, there was a slight shuffling of cloth as Michelle began to wobble on her legs – visibly weakened, and about to collapse.

That prompted Glimmer to glide over to her and place one hand upon her forehead with a *tsk-tsk* sound – transferring a jolt of magic into her body that caused her to shoot back upright once more. "Ah-uh, my dear. Not just yet. Do your mother one last favor, and kill these pests for me while I enjoy the fruits of my labor."

At first the snake girl only bowed her head. But then her body turned to the side and her golden, glowing gaze slowly rose – gliding up the rocky floor of the chamber, before locking onto her companions with an expression that was as cold as usual, but somehow far, far more unnerving and dark.

"Yes, mother."

<h1 style="text-align:center">14</h1>

All Unity and Jasper could do was stand frozen in shock as the fraught seconds drew long, and the black sand swirling around Michelle's form flared higher and higher with ominous force.

After coming all this way, and trying this hard... Is this where we lose? Was this all for nothing?

But then the snake girl's arm raised and the first blast of energy shot out towards them – leaving the wolf and the cat no time left to sink into dread, and forcing them to scramble back behind one of the last standing pillars within the now-ruined chamber, dodging blast after blast as they did so.

Once they were out of sight and range for a moment, Unity squeezed her eyes shut hard and began to plan as frantically as she could. She didn't know what to do – least of all how she could help Michelle. *Is this magic reversible? Can we even hope to take both of them? What are their weaknesses? I should have been paying so much more attention.*

Just then, however, a high-pitched sound from Jasper caused her to open her eyes. The young wolf was whimpering – glancing around neurotically, and grasping the hilt of his sword so hard that it shook visibly.

Thankfully both Michelle and Glimmer appeared to be somewhat behind in following after, and thus Unity was able to grab his shoulders and attempt to shake some sense into him. "Pooch! Calm down. We're going to fix this."

"S-Sorry..." Jasper replied, wiping at his eyes, and taking deep heaving breaths in an effort to steady himself. "It's just... I don't want to hurt her. I don't know how this happened."

"You're an adventurer, right?" Unity asked, tone steely and firm.

The wolf boy seemed surprised, but nodded. "O-of course I am!"

The cat girl furrowed her brow. "Then *be* one. Don't let them scare you. We'll get Michelle back, and kill Glimmer!"

"I wouldn't be so sure. Darling?"

Both Unity and Jasper wheeled about from their hiding spot – and just in time, too, before a blast of all too familiar dark energy caused them to leap apart, and the cat girl found herself face to face with Michelle, while Jasper soon stood below a grinning Glimmer.

Although the wolf boy could soon hear twin cries of exertion and the clash of magical forces in the distance, he had no time to look over at his two companions' fighting, and instead advanced on the floating rattlesnake in front of him – raising his sword with a still somewhat shaky hand, and steeling his expression as much as he could.

Glimmer scoffed and looked down at the young canine. "Jasper, is it?"

He nodded, and took another step forward. "That's right! I'm Jasper Carnell, from a long line of adventurers, and I'm going to stop you here and now!"

Across the other side of the room, Unity and Michelle traded magical blows at a pace even more blistering than that with which the Hustler had shot bullets – not daring to meet eyes, although Unity wasn't at all sure that Michelle herself was behind the snake girl's own.

As a result of the pace of their battle, the cat girl was already feeling the weight of energy and magic leaving her before the first minute of their battle had passed, and alongside it came the painful irony that she was now using her powers to fight against the one who had caused and helped her to discover them.

But irony would not help her now. Nor dull her horror and abject amazement when Michelle reached out with both of her scaled arms and surrounded one of the pillars which had fallen over after the Sun Skewer's explosion and flung it Unity's direction with a loud, almost pained scream. "You... I... are *nothing!*"

Only a last minute dodge and shield like the one she had used to save them from the snow kept Unity from being crushed there and then, but before she could fully right herself from the blunted impact, her eyes widened as she saw Michelle standing still upon the rocky ground just in front of her – eyes glowing gold, and black energy pouring out around her limbs, growling denser, denser, and denser, until...

The dark pressure building between them exploded all at once, and Unity was flung back faster and harder than any movement she'd ever felt – sending her crashing into the cavern's far wall, and knocking all thought and sight from her head like the snuffing out of a flame.

On the other side of the continent, Umi coasted through the skies at the edges of Penlight's boundaries on Elderex's mighty back with reins of pure magic in her hands – practicing her usual patrol to ensure that order was being held throughout the kingdom's realms.

Few other protectors of the kingdom, knights or otherwise, had skills that could rival her ability to survey large amounts of land at a time, and as such, the Queen had long since made these flights a routine. Which was something that Umi found pleasant, despite their often long and uneventful nature. Being up here away from everyone else allowed for long contemplation and peaceful thought – things she found herself lacking far too much upon the ground, surrounded by the other duties of the castle.

After reaching the northernmost end of the kingdom, where the rocks began to jut hard against the sea and only the most desolate of villages lay, Umi pulled Elderex back around and began to trace back towards Penlight Castle. A few moments later, she had arrived at its walls and towers – glistening lines and spires of stone, and within them, a thick mass of wooden buildings that seemed to grow every time she passed over them.

The opossum couldn't help but smile a little in fascination. *How the land – and people – change over time.*

Then, however, an unexpected, errant thought caught in her mind. *You know what? I should visit the Ishiis. It's been far too long since I've checked in on them, after... what happened.*

Umi guided Elderex down lower and lower in the sky, skimming over roof after roof until she pulled him to a stop altogether – causing the few citizens walking along the street beneath them to scatter as the great wyvern came to eventually rest upon cobblestone with a great flapping of wings.

The opossum dismounted from Elderex's back with a swift swing of her legs – landing herself, and glancing about to take in her surroundings as she dismissed her mount. The street was like most of the others in the city, but – most importantly - directly in front of her stood a squarish red, black, and wooden building that was still deeply familiar, despite how long she'd gone since last seeing it.

What was not familiar, however, was the sizable stack of wooden boxes out front of the Ishii Stone Shop's façade. Umi frowned just short of the door. *What's all this for? Are they shifting stock?*

A hesitant knock later, and the store's door opened in front of her – bringing her to meet the gaze of none other than Dorthroruth Ishii. The male dragon was dressed in the rough apron and cottons that she so clearly remembered him having worn back in the day, and he had a box of stone in his hands just as he'd always seemed to during the days then, but on his face...

Was none of the mirth there had once been. Instead, though recognition clearly flickered behind his eyes, Dorthro simply stood still and impassive as he came to behold Umi, and it took him quite a few seconds to speak up.

"Hello, Umi."

Then the dragon moved past her, almost forcing Umi to step back to avoid being bumped over, and set the box in his hands atop the others in front of the building before dusting off his hands.

"H-hello, Mr. Ishii. I just thought I'd drop in and see how you're doing. It's been far too long since we saw one another. Since…"

Dorthro paused in wiping off his hands, and Umi's tongue froze in turn.

Since Irin's funeral.

Another few seconds of awkward silence passed, before the dragon turned about with his gaze trained to the ground. "It's nice to see you too, one last time. Anahita and I are moving."

The opossum's head quirked to the side, and her voice piqued up in an attempt to lighten the situation. "Oh! Did you and Anahita find a new place in the city to set up shop?"

Dorthro shook his head almost angrily. "No. We're done with Penlight. We're moving. After everything that happened here…" The dragon's voice broke for a second, before he audibly wrestled it back together. "We can't keep pretending. I'm sorry."

Try as she might… Umi had no words with which to respond, and could only remain silent. Deep inside, she knew that he was right. *It's been so many years, and yet… I can still feel her absence too. Gone, just like that. Harmony's too. Maybe he's doing the right thing after all. Maybe I should do the same, even. Move on.*

As the silence wore thin, Dorthro huffed and turned away from Umi to make his way back towards the shop's door – pausing only to cast one last look over his shoulder before moving back inside.

"It was nice seeing you, Umi. I hope Unity is doing well."

Umi felt as though a dagger had struck her in the heart – leaving her standing there with tears prickling in the corners of her eyes long after the dragon had left.

After what felt like a minute, the opossum finally turned around and stretched out her arm to gather her magic – summoning Elderex back into being upon the cobblestones of the street, and making to mount up onto his back without hesitation.

"Elderex – let's leave this place."

A few breaths later the two were back up in the sky, and Unity closed her eyes against the vision of the kingdom below her - trying to use the relative peace and quiet of flying to process her thoughts. About Dorthro. About Irin. About Unity, most of all.

Before she could arrive at any conclusion or clarity, however, a powerful, dark wave of unease and force washed over her, and Umi's head jerked up with sudden, urgent alertness. *I know those powers. Far too well, just like I know how much they took. They remind me of... They were.... They are... Harmony...*

Unity.

She pulled hard on Elderex's ethereal reins – making a sharp turn in the air, and setting off at full speed towards the boundary of the kingdom, and the Arid Frontier beyond.

<h1 style="text-align:center">15</h1>

The world swam. Rocks, pillars, and the thundering magic that had been casting everything in an ethereal glow had all blended into foggy, disorienting nothingness, and all Unity could clearly feel was *pain*. In her arms, in her legs, and all across the back of her skull.

Faintly, she remembered the fight, Michelle's blows, and being knocked back – flying against the wall, while Jasper caught a piece of shrapnel and staggered to the side. But despite the weak distress that flickered in her arms at the realization that she was in danger – that Jasper was in danger – she couldn't bring herself to move or even think clearly, no matter how hard she tried.

"You're strong, Unity. I believe in you."

The voice came from nowhere, but unlike those she was used to hearing in her head, it was light and gentle, rather than dark. And familiar – calling back to times when everything had been simpler, although not perfect.

Ms. Harper.

The surprise was enough to startle Unity into raising herself to a kneel despite the pain. "Ms. Harper? I..." She coughed, waving her hand back and forth to try to get a clear glimpse through the dusty fog surrounding her. "I failed. I'm sorry."

The voice came again. "No, Unity. You won't fail. Not now, and not ever. Come – show them what you have in you."

Unity closed her eyes hard, blurring out the pain, the fear, and the dread...

And began to rise. Her hands tented her upwards, her legs straightened, and she furrowed her brow with resolve. "Jasper? Michelle? I-"

The cat girl cut herself short, shaking her head. *Michelle... shouldn't hear me. I don't want to hurt her, but right now I just need to move fast, find Jasper, and come up with a plan.*

Stepping forward blindly, Unity continued to swirl the dust around her about with her hand, and eventually began to make her way out of the cloud of debris that Michelle's blast had created.

But then, with her first reorienting glances out at what remained of the Sun Skewer's chamber, was when she saw him. Crumpled on his side, with his muzzle wedged hard into the stony ground.

Ignoring the echoes of pain and fatigue wracking her body just as she had after the explosion that had destroyed the orphanage, Unity sprung to instinctive action – scrambling first over to where Jasper lay, and then down on her knees.

As she got her first glance at the young wolf's form and the light slick of blood seeping through the side of his jerkin, the weight in the pit of her stomach deepened yet further, and for the first time since starting their adventure, she felt fear. *Real* fear.

They'd made it through so much in this past week or more – come so close to danger and doom so many times in such a short breath... to fall now, to lose *him* of all people now... felt unfitting. Anticlimactic. Stupid.

The cat girl squeezed her eyes shut. *Back then I hated every moment of his stupid, optimistic chatter, but if he's gone... I don't know what else to keep doing this for. We wouldn't have gotten this far without him.*

Before terror could cloud her mind further, however, or she could properly ascertain whether Jasper had stopped breathing, there was a sharp crackle of energy from the center of the chamber, and she turned to see Glimmer emerging from amongst the fog with the scepter glowing in her hand and Michelle at her side – gliding just above the ground atop orbs of golden magic.

The rattlesnake spread her arms wide and smirked. "There you are. Still standing – impressive." Her gaze wandered down to the prone body in front of Unity, and she tilted her head. "Afraid the same can't be said for your friend. Shame.

But now I can finish you off and have this perfect, perfect prize all to myself. Michelle?"

Unity backed up – putting herself between Michelle and Jasper as best as she could, and preparing her last energy reserves to ward off an attack. The longer the seconds stretched, however, the more the tension and fear the cat girl had felt diffused, until Glimmer frowned and raised the Sun Skewer in her daughter's direction. "Michelle – obey."

But the snake girl still remained frozen, and – after a few seconds more – began to slowly shake her head. "No."

Glimmer's eyes shot wide. "You wouldn't dare."

At that very moment, however, Michelle's arms spread out, she let a high, almost pained shriek, and a great burst of dark energy shot out from her in all directions – dispelling the gold from her eyes and form.

Immediately after, while Glimmer was forced to step back and reflexively raise the Skewer to defend herself, Michelle collapsed to her knees, and Unity immediately rushed over. The snake girl waved her away with one hand, however, while supporting herself upon the floor with her other.

"Unity, I..." She shook her head. "The Skewer. Its shield. It's drained me. My powers are coming back, but... too slowly. I can't fight. Not anymore."

The cat girl opened her mouth to respond, but then Glimmer was advancing from behind her, hefting the Sun Skewer high. "Enough. You choose betrayal? Then you will die, just like them. Just like all those who have forsaken me."

As the rattlesnake drew nearer, however, Unity failed to flinch. Instead, she came fully to face Glimmer, moved forward as well, and extended one hand to summon her long, silver-black blade – ignoring the tangible drain she felt as a result. "First you kill Ms. Harper, and take away the only home I have. Then you call yourself a mother to Michelle after all of this – after *using* her. And now you do this to Jasper?"

Glimmer watched the cat girl form her blade and focus her power with one eyebrow quirked, but nothing but confidence was written upon her face. "Fool. I've waited far too long for this. Suffered too much. Upholder and her house of deceit hold no qualms of tossing aside and taking what they need to see out their will, so neither will I. To stand in my way is to die – so that what needs to be done may be done."

Slowly, coldly, Unity shook her head. "No – *you* will die." She turned over her shoulder to Michelle, where the snake woman still knelt by Jasper's form. "I have this, Michelle. Take care of him."

Michelle nodded, and the cat girl turned back around to face her opponent, who was already raising the Sun Skewer in turn.

Like a vicious, frantic dance, Glimmer and Unity began to lash out and unleash blasts of magic in one another's direction – causing the chamber to shake with each new gold or black explosion.

Michelle's magic and blows had been powerful, but where Unity had been able to challenge their strength, she was soon to realize that trying to directly deflect or shield herself against blasts from the Sun Skewer would mean certain death. *I'm going to have to be smart about this, and I'm going to have to find a way fast.*

The longer that she and Glimmer sparred, however, the sloppier and angrier the serpent woman's moves became, and the more and more she cried out and snarled each time she summoned energy through the Skewer. Unity had always supposed that Michelle's relative lack of outward emotion had been a quirk related to her species, but with realizing that she'd been wrong... she also realized that she'd found her opening.

The idea was stupid, and she knew it, but there was also no time for thought. So, as Glimmer wheeled about to let out another blast of energy, she let the impulse catch her, and...

Stuck out her tongue.

The rattlesnake's eyes flared even wider than they had before, and she let out a deep, thundering roar that brought a great crackle of golden energy to lash out around her dark robes. "You will *die!*"

Levelling both the Sun Skewer and a free hand pulsating with her own magic, Glimmer's shoulders bridged high, and she began to unleash wave after wave of mixed, volatile power.

But Unity was faster, and more collected. The power of the Skewer was absolute, but Glimmer's aim and coordination was degrading by the moment – leaving the cat girl just enough room to work her way closer and closer, upping the tempo of their duel higher and higher – causing more and more blasts to ricochet and blast chunks of the cavern down and away. Faster, faster, and faster, until...

Almost uneventfully, Unity lunged forward, and it happened. The cat girl's increasingly unstable magic blade caught the Skewer beneath its hooked tip, and it was wrenched from Glimmer's hands – causing the snake woman to hiss sharply and lunge forward in an effort to catch it.

But what was done was done. The skewer clattered to the ground near where Jasper laid and Michelle was kneeling to tend to him, and Glimmer's desperate grasping succeeded only in causing her to stumble forward and fall to the ground with a dull thud.

The rattlesnake soon twisted about and attempted to pull herself back up, but Unity was faster – lashing out with her powers to pin both of her wrists up in the air, cutting the lashes of gold energy already arcing up Glimmer's arms short.

"Not this time." The cat girl took a step forward and pulled forward sharply with her magic – causing Ms. Harper's killer to collapse to her knees.

For a moment Glimmer simply huffed and struggled, trying to summon her own powers again and again, before her gaze turned frantic, and she looked over to Michelle, who was watching the scene unfold with her hands clasped upon Jasper's wounded side.

"Michelle. Please. Give me the Skewer." She shook her head urgently, voice cracking with nerves. "I can make this right. I can keep you safe. We can take what's ours – together."

Yet Michelle's expression remained unchanged, and the younger snake simply shrugged. "No."

That made Glimmer spit, and jerk her head back up towards Unity. "This is all because of you. Your mother. Your cursed, disgusting blood."

Unity's mind froze to a sudden, stunned halt. Her jaw dropped, and when her voice came, it was as timid and shaky as Glimmer's had been. "My mother?"

Glimmer spat again, but Unity snapped out of her initial shock and jolted her arms forward again, causing the magic bonds around the snake before her to tug her closer to the ground. "Enough. Tell me why you're doing this. Tell me about my mother."

The rattlesnake huffed indignantly. "She was a worthless slave, just like you. Although, you don't even know it, do you?"

Unity responded to that by dipping her magical blade a good few inches closer to Glimmer's throat, and lowering her voice to a fearsome growl. "Tell me."

"She was a *monster*. She killed my husband Archer like it was nothing." The rattlesnake was practically snarling every word by now. "And Upholder allowed it. Allowed it! Just like the deaths of so many others. Because it befitted her great 'plan'. But look where it got her – look where it got your mother."

Suddenly looking deeply, bitterly satisfied, Glimmer stared right into Unity's eyes, and her pupils began to glow an even deeper, richer gold. "She died, and Upholder will die too – I'll see to it."

But Unity was done listening. Letting out a deep roar of her own, she drew back her blade, lined it straight, and drove it forward through the rattlesnake's chest – causing Glimmer to gasp in shock, and the golden glow to fade from the corners of her eyes like the snuffing of a flame.

Before the rattlesnake could begin her death throes, however, Unity suddenly felt her head swimming, and her vision began to blur. As such, as Glimmer crumpled to the side, so did she – falling to her knees just before black consumed everything around her.

The cat girl could see nothing in that dark void, but she could feel *everything*. Past, present, and future. Souls, dark burning wells like her. Countless lives taken, just like that which she had now. *This has happened before. It will happen again. You may have won for now, you may have killed her... but she's right, and you know it.*

She was slipping, she could feel it. The voices were louder than ever before, and their words soon began to bleed into one another – merging into and amplifying one another until her entire brain was filled with deafening humming.

Unity.

With that voice, teetering on the very edge of darkness, she felt Michelle's hand on her shoulder. Just like it in the forest, after Ms. Harper had just fallen, and her pledge to take revenge had been fresh.

Slowly, painstakingly, she began to claw herself back to consciousness – focusing first on the stone floor beneath her knees, then on the pain of her various bruises, and finally on the blurry sight of Glimmer's slumped body that was slowly forming in front of her.

"Unity. I'm here."

The cat girl finally blinked and fully resumed control of her body – letting the full intensity of the scene rush in at once. Not only did the chamber stink of smoke and ozone from the sheer strength of the magic that had been released within it, but it was all but completely dark now – except for a few small holes in the ceiling which seemed to let through small beams of daylight.

Unable to look down at the robed corpse in front of her nor the blood pooling beneath it that she had caught a half-glimpse of for fear of slipping back into the dark, Unity instead looked back up at Michelle with a shaky, vulnerable smile. "Thank you. I... don't know what would have happened."

The snake girl nodded with her usual neutral nature – which was almost impossibly relieving to see after her previous possession - but then glanced over her shoulder, and gestured with her thumb. "Jasper's awake."

Unity stood up with an impulsive suddenness that both surprised her and brought a cry of unexpectedly piercing agony to run through her limbs. *Ouch. Need to take it a bit slower than that.*

But then she spotted Jasper's form, and darted over to where the young wolf was slowly pulling himself up to a kneel. "Jasper! You're okay, I-"

The joy of having finally made it and the relief of Jasper being alright melded into one, and she swooped down with her body and head without thinking – bringing their lips to meet.

At first Jasper's eyes flared wide and his wounded body stiffened, but then he let a rush of air out of his nose, and returned Unity's abandon and enthusiasm – holding her close from where he lay.

And in that moment, despite the aching of her entire body, the fatigue of having used so much magic, the blood matting Jasper's side and the countless cuts of Unity's own... despite everything they'd been through together in this past week...

It felt like it had all been worth it after all.

16

— ∙ —

It felt like forever before they were able to collect themselves, check their limbs fully for injuries, and catch their breath amongst the rubble that had once been the fairly well-kept chamber, but eventually they had themselves back on their feet, and set about leaving the chamber as quickly as they could in fear of the damage done to it eventually causing a cave-in. Which, from the parts of the falling debris that occasionally clattered down about their heads, wasn't all that unlikely.

It'd been strange leaving Glimmer's body there where she had fallen – after Jasper had retrieved his family's map from her person, of course - but somewhere inside, Unity took a kind of satisfaction knowing that she'd be buried where she had so desperately fought and schemed to go.

The Sun Skewer, however, had been nowhere to be seen. Unity couldn't remember glimpsing it since before she had nearly succumbed to the dark, and Michelle said that it had simply vanished sometime after the fight.

There's a kind of justice to that. She did make it and achieve her goal, after all. She did what she promised her husband. And the Skewer is still with her... somewhere.

It took them longer to emerge from the caverns than it had for them to enter without Glimmer's magic and the scepter to sniff after, as well as due to the fact that Michelle was still recovering from the drain of dispelling the shield and her possession, but thankfully Jasper's uncanny memory prevailed once more, and they emerged where they had started before midday had properly left the sky.

A few minutes later, and they were back within Guardright's limits, where daily work seemed to be settling down a little, and folks were visible idly chatting all across the street and at various establishments as the battered and dusty three made their way through. The air of normalcy was unbelievably strange, after their battle within the mountains. *If only they knew we found it after all. That the Sun Skewer wasn't a legend after all.*

Just as the reality of the fact that they were free had truly begun to settle in, however, for good and bad, something that none of them could have seen coming came to pass. A great, deafening thrumming began to emanate above the street they stood on – causing the town's denizens to scatter and run into houses.

Stuck with nowhere to run to and too exhausted to react at speed, however, Unity, Jasper, and Michelle could only stand still and glance around in confusion – until the cat girl's gaze eventually turned upwards and widened. A great, two-legged dragon was slowly descending out of the air just in front of them – and as it came closer and closer to the ground, the gusts of air it brought made it harder and harder for the trio to keep their feet.

Eventually the beast finally touched ground, and a leather-clad figure slid from its back to land with a dull thud of boots upon cobblestone. It was an opossum – gray-furred, violet-eyed, and matter-of-fact in manner as she strode towards them and nodded in greeting.

"Children – I'm sorry to provide such a sudden greeting. But are you..." The mysterious woman's eyes lingered on Unity. "Unity Mei?"

The cat girl responded only by narrowing her eyes. "Who are you?"

A long moment passed in relative silence as the wyvern stirred, and the opossum's face rose and fell with an unidentifiable mix of emotions. "I take that as a yes. You have your mother's directness." Her face split with a weak smile. "And you are strong like her, too. I can sense that you have fought hard, and won harder today."

Unity's frown deepened, and she tented one hand on her hip. "You haven't answered my question."

The opossum sighed – seeming awfully awkward despite her noble posture and armor. "Right, right. My name is Umi. I am... a knight of Penlight. As was your mother."

That wiped Unity's face clean, and caused Michelle and Jasper to glance over at her in shock. But the mysterious arrival wasn't done. "We were together. When she had you, when she died... and trusted me with your care."

Another moment of silence, before Umi nodded, and bit her lip. "For now – if it suits you, I can offer fast passage back to Penlight, and I can tell you the rest along the way. You must not endanger yourself any longer than you have been forced to, before I could find you"

Unity was still too shocked to provide an answer, so Jasper looked back to the opossum and spoke up instead. "What kind of fast passage do you mean?"

Again allowing the lightest twinge of a smile to touch the edge of her lip, Umi extended her leather-clad arm, and deep purple magic began to form within her palm.

"Let me show you."

Once Jasper's initial enthusiasm and bewilderment at first seeing and then climbing into the sky with Elderex had subsided, the trio rode silently behind Umi on the wyvern's back – watching the land and clouds beneath them pass by in silence.

All the while, half of Unity's mind grappled with powerful anger. This gutless woman had abandoned her, and had only come back now, after everything she'd been through and survived. But the other half was... simply numb. It was over. Glimmer was defeated. Even Umi's arrival and learning who she was had barely sunk in.

Eventually they flew over what even Unity recognized as the edge of the bay under which they had travelled, and it was then that Jasper tentatively broke the silence between them. "Mrs. Unity?"

Umi chuckled, though she kept her head facing forward and her hands on Elderex's neck. "You can call me Umi."

Jasper chuckled, seeming nervous but still a little excited. "We have a friend just down there – at the edge of the bay. Would you mind taking her with us to Penlight? She doesn't have a home."

The opossum nodded, and started to guide her summon into a descent. "Anything. You've been alone for far too long."

It took them something like twenty minutes to find the axolotl girl amongst the sand and rocks – crouched down and shivering a little from Elderex's understandably intimidating arrival – but once she recognized Unity, Michelle, and Jasper, the lattermost was easily able to convince her to travel with them. They weren't exactly sure what kind of life they could offer her – or what awaited them, even – but they knew it would be better than a solitary life scavenging on the coast, and it seemed that Bubbles agreed.

Later, as they drew further and further into the evening sun, and the orange-cast silhouette of Penlight Castle became visible on the horizon, Unity had never felt more uncertain about what was waiting for her – them – now that their quest was at an end, especially after her kiss with Jasper and the flutters of confusion that idea still stirred within her chest, but she knew one thing.

If she'd overcome this – all the challenges and danger they'd faced over the last weeks – then nothing could scare her anymore. Be it monsters, be it loneliness, be it the rage and voices inside her head -

She could overcome anything.

EPILOGUE

Six years later

In many ways, the years that followed Unity, Michelle, and Jasper's quest to save the Sun Skewer from Glimmer's hands were like any other. The winters came and passed, the fields flourished, and the folk went about their rituals and trades with the same tireless dedication that they had ever since their births at Ophin's hands.

Yet in others, they were years of great change. Most of all, perhaps, when it came to the kingdom's royal family. Justice and Amethyst finished their training, came into their own as knights of Penlight, and, as their successful quests and achievements grew exponentially, were soon properly announced as the heirs apparent to the throne - set to mutually rule over the kingdom when the time came.

As for the adventuring trio themselves – despite their newfound belief in themselves and Unity's powers, neither she nor Michelle and Bubbles had a home to return to, and as such, stayed with Jasper's mother and father until they came of age, and could get their own houses.

Under these circumstances, it didn't take long for the growing fondness between Unity and Jasper to blossom into love, and that love to blossom into a deep, meaningful connection long after they left the house for a place of their own with the help of Jasper's father.

Speaking of connections - Unity kept contact with Umi, as well. Although, perhaps not as closely as Umi might have hoped. The cat girl was reluctant, at first, to discuss much of her life or reveal much of herself to her mother's lover, but some say that time bridges all gaps – and as the years went on, the two maintained a regular stream of letters and occasional visits.

Eventually, Jasper and Unity's love grew into the birth of something new altogether, and two fresh Mei children – twins – were born under the care of Mystic and the castle's other healing practitioners. Unity named the first child, her daughter, Trinity, whereas Jasper named the second child, their son, Empathy. Both had gray fur, but patches of white across their face, and beneath their eyes.

Some time later, once the pair had settled back into their home after the birth and Unity had returned to full strength, the two took a trip out to the rural villages to visit Michelle and Bubbles' house - which had also been granted to them with Jasper's father's help.

By the time that they arrived at the village dwelling, with Unity holding Empathy in her arms and Jasper cradling Trinity, the afternoon sun had begun to crest across the trees of the forest just behind its roof – reminding the cat woman suddenly of the day she'd met Michelle. *It feels so long ago – like another world. Nothing remains of then. Not Ms. Harper, not the orphanage...*

And not who I used to be. I'm stronger, now.

Freeing up one arm from beneath Trinity, Jasper knocked on the dwelling's door with his tail wagging eagerly behind him. Unity rolled her eyes, but before she could make a jokingly disparaging comment about her husband's indomitable eagerness for social occasions, a latch shifted, and the threshold in front of them cleared to reveal a snake woman wearing a long black cloak.

That made Unity's mood darken somewhat, and her expression alongside it. *She's wearing that robe again. Her work is noble, yes, but it reminds me of Glimmer. Glimmer, and the dreams...*

But then Michelle was smiling in her usual measured, cold way, and beckoning them inside. "Unity, Jasper. And the babies. They look like they've already grown since I last visited. Come – Bubbles is so excited."

Jasper obeyed without waiting even a second, and immediately struck up idle chatter with Michelle while Unity was left to follow after, allowing the door to close behind them. The hallway beyond was quite rustic and narrow, but the space soon opened up into a quite large sitting area, where a few wooden chairs and a long couch ran along the wall.

It was in the chair closest to the door at the other end of the room, which likely led to a kitchen, that a familiar axolotl sat – wearing a robe much like Michelle was, and beaming from cheek to cheek with eagerness. Bubbles sprung up the moment that the two new arrivals came into sight, and was soon flitting between the children they held with various squeaks of enthusiasm. "They're so adorable! Thank you so much for letting us meet them!"

Jasper smiled just as widely as Bubbles. "Of course! Who knows if we'd even be around today if it weren't for your help. Both of you."

Bubbles giggled. "That's nonsense. But if you need a babysitter, you know where to find one!"

Michelle was stood off to the side with her slender arms crossed in front of her robe, and nodded at this while Bubbles continued to coo over the babies. "I could say the same to you. But that brings me to exciting news of our own. The Queen has declared her support and funding for our work."

Jasper's jaw fell open, and he hugged Trinity closer to this chest. "And that means..?"

The snake woman nodded. "That we'll be able to reopen Penlight Orphanage. With some changes, of course. I don't want other children with abilities to grow up fearing their powers like I did. And the Queen seems to agree."

Jasper beamed at that and peppered Michelle with a barrage of further whens and hows, but Unity found herself drifting away from the conversation, and further into her thoughts with each minute. Her thoughts, and her memories.

Upholder allowed it. Just like the deaths of so many others. Because it befitted her great 'plan'. But look where it got her – look where it got your mother.

In the evening after arriving back from Michelle and Bubbles' house, Unity and Jasper wasted no time in setting themselves to preparing for rest. Days were short and nights were long thanks to the twins' constant need for care, and Unity herself was already feeling the dull pull of sleep by the time that she and her husband made their way to their own bedroom after laying the children to bed.

Their house, which had been gifted to them by Titan as a wedding gift, was large, fairly ornate, and located amongst the castle's outer walls – just central enough to be safe and close to any services that they might need, and just isolated enough to give the new family some peace and quiet.

Unity and Jasper's personal bedroom was also large and ornate, at least as large as the dormitory hall that Unity had spent her first sixteen years in and of itself, and housed a fine wooden bed with a plush feather mattress.

It was this bed that cradled the cat girl softly as she settled back into it – letting out a deep sigh, and watching idly as Jasper rounded the bed, stretching out his arms with a suppressed yawn. The both of them were still dressed in their outside clothes, but neither had the energy necessary to change out and back into sleepwear, and so Jasper wasted no time in settling down next to his wife and shuffling back against the headboard.

As soon as her husband was positioned next to her, Unity closed her eyes and did her best to prepare for rest. She had a piercing, dark headache forming between her brows – as she had all too often these days – and sleep was the only thing that could give her a moment of relief.

That's if the dreams don't-

The cat girl's head shot straight up where she was slumped as the sharp, instinct-tugging sound of crying perforated the air from the adjacent nursery. *Or that.*

Unity couldn't help but groan out loud in a mixture of frustration, pain, and even a faint flicker of anger. "Again? Ophin..."

"Another headache?" Frowning with worry, Jasper reached over to gently run a hand along Unity's forehead, before hopping up from the bed and beginning to make towards the bedroom's door. "Don't worry, I'll handle them. You just try to get some rest, alright?"

She frowned, but nodded. "I'll try."

As her husband turned to leave the room, however, an even sharper jab of agony shot through her skull, and she cried out – causing Jasper to turn around with a huff of concern.

"No, wait. I need a moment to freshen up." The cat girl shook her head and started to hastily climb out of bed. *I can't do this anymore – I need to try something.*

Looking even more worried, Jasper nodded and cautiously continued through the doorway. "Sounds great. Take your time. I'll calm the kids down, and wait up for you."

The two parted ways in the hall, with Jasper heading into the nursery and Unity continuing a little longer until she came to the bathroom and shut herself inside.

The space's interior was fairly plain – lined on one side by a set of two gas lamps, and fitted with a washtub and basin on the other – and she walked over to the lattermost to look over her tired, worn face in the mirror above it until she felt as though she could start to see her eyes get redder the longer she looked. *It's all so much... and it will never end. I know it won't. It'll be just day after day of this, and-*

A shadow flittered just out of sight in the mirror's reflection, and Unity's heart jumped into her throat as she spun around in the gas-lit room to find nothing behind her.

Gritting her teeth, the cat woman growled and looked to the room door. "Jasper? This isn't the time to mess with me. Come out."

No response came, leaving her to sigh and go back to the mirror. "I'm just stressed, and need to sleep. Maybe in the morning I ask Michelle whether she'll watch the kids after all."

But then a hand clasped upon her shoulder. Cold, with sharp, jagged fingers that dug deep until they felt as though they might draw blood.

Whirling around with a growl already on her teeth and magic power already forming black within her hands, Unity lashed out at the hand's owner with all of her might, only to find...

Nothing. Dissipating, wafting smoke.

Her shock and confusion had no time to take effect, however, before the dark fog took form again. A tall, skinny mass with countless arms and legs, stood across from her at the other end of the room, and staring down with glowing red eyes.

Unity's heart stopped. *What is... Is this...*

The figure lashed forward with both of its arms at once – letting out an unearthly screech that echoed on and on as the cat woman deflected the strikes with magical shields.

The two soon ended up trading blows at a blistering pace, with Unity barely able to breathe or process a single thought between anticipation, action, and instinct. As such, it took her a moment to realize that she was defending herself no longer against just one intangible opponent, but two. Then three, then four, and then more than she could count.

The tight space of the bathroom almost seemed to swell to contain them and their combat, as though this were all some cruel, twisted dream, but Unity's energy failed to expand with it. After what felt like the longest minute of the cat woman's life, her chest was aching more sharply than she could ever remember, and her cries of exertion were turning into pants of desperation. *I can't do this. I'm slipping, I don't know what's happening. And... and...*

And yet somehow, as she teetered right on the border of desperation...

It all clicked within her mind. The voices. The magic. This *curse*.

She saw this for what it was, now. Not something without, but something within her. This was what she'd been born to fight. And fight it she would – forever, if she had to. For Jasper. For Michelle. For everyone who had ever shown her faith.

Letting out a shrill, powerful roar, Unity cast her arms back with as much force as she could muster. And, as she did so, a great wave of energy radiated out from her figure - shattering the walls and roof of her 'house' away into nothing but smoke, and revealing a gray, featureless, dreamlike plain behind them.

Swarms upon swarms of the dark, shadowy beasts rolled forth across her desolate surroundings, but she felt nothing but a burst of determination and fury at the sight - sinking back into a fighting stance, and bearing her teeth.

"Come at me, bastards! I'm not letting you take me down – ever!"

Back in the real world, outside the prison of her mind, Unity hunched forward over the basin – her eyes glowing gray, and an aura of dark, viscous energy seeping out into the air about her body.

But as actively as the hungry darkness seemed to push and surge, it did not expand, and it did not consume her. The gray energy within her was stronger – pushing it back on all fronts with steady, glowing strength.

She would fight this. She was strong. She was different.

She was Unity, and she could overcome anything.